The Eagle and the P

The Eagle
and
the Phoenix

Coventry Stories for Young People

Sheila Woolf

With illustrations by David R Clarke

This edition published 2020 by:
Takahe Publishing Ltd.
Registered Office:
77 Earlsdon Street, Coventry CV5 6EL

ISBN 978-1-908837-17-2

Illustrations © David R Clarke 2020

TAKAHE PUBLISHING LTD. 2020

For all Coventry Kids, real or imagined, past, present and future.

vi

Acknowledgements

So many people have written about Coventry's history that my bookshelves are groaning with all their books. As a result I must say thank you to them all for their inspiration. In recent years, too, it has been a delight to browse websites such as www.historiccoventry.co.uk as well as many Facebook pages set up by enthusiasts for the city's past. It's good to realise how many people still engage in the stories which such a great city can tell.

Lots of people encouraged me to write this book, and I owe a special debt to early readers Helen Childs and Nathalia Perera, and to Peter James who spurred me on when I was flagging. The story about the November Blitz is inspired by the account written at the end of the Second World War by the late Arthur Higgens, and I am grateful to his family for allowing me to make it available.

Steven Hodder has brought his expertise to the publication, making a reality out of what began as an idea many years ago; my thanks to him.

Lastly, Dave Clarke, usually known as DRC to countless young aspiring artists, provided illustrations every bit as lively as I knew he would – thanks, Darce!

Sheila Woolf

Contents

Preface

Have you ever wondered what it would be like to be growing up in Coventry in the past?

- When Romans camped nearby, at the Lunt Fort,

- When Godiva made her famous "naked" journey through the streets, in Saxon times,

- When Coventry's medieval "mystery plays" inspired a young William Shakespeare,

- When kings and queens in Tudor times were regular visitors,

- When the "Coventry Blitz" destroyed the city centre and its great cathedral in World War Two.

Join Marcus, Edith, Sally, Amit and many more, as they tell the stories of some of the dramatic moments in Coventry's long and fascinating history – and imagine yourself there.

CHAPTER ONE

Friend and Roman

Around the year AD 60 the Roman army had been victorious over the British Iceni tribe at the Battle of Mancetter – not far from Coventry. Twelve miles away from Mancetter, at Baginton, on a hillside above today's Coventry, was a Roman settlement, where they established a fort – the Lunt Fort.

Here they constructed a feature which is unique in northern Europe – a circular area called a gyrus, where the Romans brought the horses they had captured from the British, and trained them for Roman military use. The fort fell into disuse many years ago, but in the twentieth century it was reconstructed, and it is still possible to stand in the gyrus and recapture the memory of that training procedure. The shape of the structure provides echoes which multiply sound. Just a few claps of the hand will sound like a lot of noise, and you can imagine the soldiers beating their shields to get the horses used to the sound of battle.

The stallion's eyes rolled hideously, the whites tinged with red veins, the pupils seeming to Marcus as though they were darting black fire. The horse's magnificent flanks shuddered, glistening with great rivers of sweat as his hooves seared angrily into the dust beneath. Marcus stood his ground and clashed his sword against his shield once more, this time dangerously close to the animal's head above him. The steel flashed and the horse veered away.

"You will obey me!" Marcus screamed. "Listen to the battle-sound – it will not harm you!" His shouts echoed around the gyrus, suddenly sounding like twenty voices rebounding from all the timber surfaces. He clapped his hands repeatedly, and the horse flinched from the sounds he could hear exploding from all sides towards his head. Small flecks of spittle foamed from his mouth. Suddenly he stood still.

"That's good, my beauty," said Marcus. "You'll be all right, trust me. All I want for you is that you'll not be frightened when you hear the real noise of battle. A Roman horse must be steady, loyal and proud to carry his rider to victory."

The horse breathed heavily as he shook his head as if to dislodge the awful sounds. He and Marcus looked steadily at each other. For a moment, Marcus felt as if the horse might speak. What might it say? – was he more angry than sad, that he had been taken away from the open fields, forced to carry goods for Boudica's army and was now a captive of the conquering Romans? Was he more afraid of imprisonment, here at the Lunt Fort, than he would be of taking part in future battles?

"That's enough for today," Marcus told him, and prepared to lead him back to the stables close by. As he slipped through the gate of the gyrus, quickly closing it behind him and nodding to the man in the holding area to open the horses' gate, he thought soberly of how these magnificent British captives must long for the chance to gallop free, instead of being shut up for long periods of time in between their training sessions in the gyrus.

"Are you missing your fields then, lad? Do you hope to go back to them one day, to serve your British masters? We all have our dreams, but you can change your dreams, you know. What about a dream of playing a part in the great Roman army – what about helping the Roman Empire?" Marcus chattered on to the horse as he dried him off in the stable, sensing that he was listening to what Marcus was saying.

"You know, Vitus, we're not so very different, you and I," said Marcus. He, too, had left his native land, the glorious sunny hillsides of Italy, and had travelled in search of adventure since then. He had almost stopped wondering whether he would ever go home again – the army was his family now, and he had found adventures, which were more than compensation for the quiet olive groves of home. He still found himself remembering, as he slipped into sleep, the sight of his mother and sister waving and crying as he left, promising that he would return as a senator at least. "I have changed my dream, certainly," he thought. "Now all I want is a good night's sleep, enough corn-bread in my belly and a heap of savings for my future. One day I shall go home and buy a farm; with these savings and the plot of land the army will give me, I'll be allowed to keep an old unwanted horse or two as well."

Horses were the reason Marcus had found himself at the Lunt Fort, right in the heart of England. Knowing him to be a farm boy, used to animals, one of the centurions had asked for him to remain there after the Battle of Mancetter. What a wonderful day that had been, when they had defeated the feared Boudica, Queen of the British Iceni tribe! Not only was it a famous victory, after the British had caused so much harm to the Romans who had settled in Britain, but they had captured hundreds of the tribe's horses, and had brought them here to the Lunt to be trained as part of the Roman cavalry. Marcus had been given the best job of his young life so far, breaking in the spirited creatures in the gyrus.

He was so proud of this great Roman invention – and what's more, it was the only one of its kind in the northern lands of the Roman Empire. A perfect circle of tall timbers within the ramparts of the fort, it enabled single sounds to be magnified and multiplied so that noise made by only a few people sounded as if huge crowds were there. Marcus and other young men would shout, clap hands and clang swords, and the noise would echo around to imitate the awful din of battle. Horses were transformed from mere wagon-pullers into the fearless war-horses the Roman army needed.

That night Marcus prayed, and made sacrifices to his personal gods. He had wandered the fort after his brief meal of vegetable broth, and had played a few games of dice with the other lads before lining up for his pay, depositing some as savings as the army required. Climbing up to the ramparts he looked across the valley below, towards scattered settlements beneath the fort, and heard the horses whinnying softly to each other in the stable block. Suddenly he was aware of the soft rustle of someone's cloak. Turning, he was surprised to see the Praetor's wife, Helena, the only woman permitted to live within the fort. The Praetor's quarters were spacious, and it was rare for any of the fort's other occupants to set eyes upon Helena. She was unhappy living in Britain, with its cold, wet climate, and longed to return to the warmth of home. Marcus wasn't quite sure what to say to her.

"A beautiful night, isn't it?" the lady said. "Look at those stars in the southern sky. If you try hard, you can imagine another land beneath them – our land. Our grass is just as green as these hillsides, and our woods just as thickly spread. But we have the advantage of sunshine, haven't we? How wonderful it would be to wake up to a sunny morning for a change, with the cicadas crackling and the swifts whirling! I am tired of the rain, the fog in that valley down there, and the coarse sound of crows and rooks. When do you think you'll be going home, boy?"

"Not until I'm an old man, I expect," said Marcus wistfully.

"Poor boy! After you've spent years in the company of old men and horses, to go back to your hills a wise but irritable veteran, limping with rheumatism and scarred from battle? What a life!" sighed Helena.

"It's an honourable life, gladly given to my legion and the Empire," retorted Marcus. He realised straight away how pompous his words sounded. But it was too late.

"Pardon me, young man," replied Helena sarcastically. "I did not intend to criticise the greatness of Rome. But I cannot help thinking that a young man like you should be with his family on his own farm, enjoying the sunshine of Italy." And with that, she turned and left.

Marcus was unsettled. He began to think of home and of the animals he loved. He loved the horses here too, but he knew they would leave the fort as soon as training was over, and he would see them no more. Returning to his sleeping quarters, he got himself ready to sleep, with a vivid image in his mind of the farm at home and the warmth of the sun.

In his dream, the wind was blowing in his hair. The trees' boughs were creaking and their leaves rustling, and the smell of smoke from burning olive wood was sharp in his nostrils. He could hear horses restlessly stirring in their stables and some strange, unidentifiable sounds in the distance, too.

Suddenly he snapped himself awake. He looked around in the dim light. He was not at home and dreaming, as it had seemed, but here in cold Britain, the smell of soldiers and armour all around him. But what was that sound? Marcus rubbed his eyes. Suddenly he had it – he could hear Vitus. He could recognise that horse's sounds as well as a mother knows her child's cries.

Marcus threw off the warm straw which covered him, and hurried to the door. What he saw outside he could scarcely believe: there stood Vitus, shaking his mane and pawing the ground impatiently. He swerved away when Marcus appeared, his eyes rolling frantically. Marcus looked up at the night sky, seeing the low clouds covering the gatehouse at the ramparts. But wait! These were not clouds, so low as to obscure the top of the sentry-posts – it was smoke! So Marcus' dream of smoke had come to him from the real world – the whole timber structure of the fort had begun to catch fire!

Marcus ran round to the stables, where he saw how Vitus had kicked open the door. The other horses jostled each other inside, and Marcus could smell their terror. Now they made a move to break out through the open door, sensing that the fire was as yet on the opposite side of the fort. But Vitus had come to alert Marcus – to save his life and perhaps that of the fort itself.

Marcus rushed to where the sentry should be. He could just make out in the darkness the shape of a man, slumped in a corner. He must have been overcome by the smoke, before he could let others know of the danger. Marcus thought quickly. There was no time to go across to the barracks – he must wake the Praetor himself.

He hurried to a rear door and banged on it, shouting at the top of his lungs and feeling them already taking in the sharp smoke. To his surprise, it was Helena who answered the door. "Wake the camp! The fort is on fire at the gatehouse! The sentry may be dead!" he yelled, hardly knowing what he was saying.

When it was all over, Marcus only barely remembered what happened during the rest of that night. He could recall Vitus, amazingly, returning to the stables, as though once he had awakened Marcus his job was done. Men swarmed over the fort, carrying water from the nearby river, and before too long the fire was out, the sentry revived, and Marcus was seated in front of a very weary Praetor, with Helena offering him water to drink.

"We have to thank you, my lad, for your prompt action," said the Praetor. "We might all have been burnt in our beds but for your quick thinking."

"Don't thank me, it was Vitus who did the thinking," Marcus replied quickly, and told the Praetor of Vitus's actions.

"And are you such close friends, your Vitus and you?" the Praetor enquired with a smile. "I did not realise that boys and horses spoke the same language!"

"I have watched this boy training the horses in the gyrus," interrupted Helena, "while I have been taking a walk on the ramparts – it's clear that he and the horses have a particular understanding. I have seen him succeed in calming them when others have tried and failed. He is good enough to be with Caesar's horses, not spending his time here in this miserable place. It will soon be time for the legion to leave; what will he do then? Write to your brother in Rome, husband – he has influence with Caesar – and ask if he has need of good horse-trainers."

Marcus looked from Helena to the Praetor and back again, and felt that everything in his life was about to change.

"Very well, my dear," the Praetor said. "Why not? Letters will be sent. Would you like that, my boy?"

Marcus could scarcely believe his ears. To be in Rome, to be employed by the Emperor, to work with the best horses in the known world...

"He'll need a horse, you realise," said Helena, with a wink towards Marcus.

Later that night Marcus walked across to the stables, and sat for a while with Vitus. The horse was calm now, and looked steadily at him. Again Marcus had the feeling that if the horse were to speak aloud, he would not be surprised.

"So we're to go, Vitus. Yours will be a new life, serving Rome too. You will never see your native fields again, no matter how much you will dream of them."

As he stroked the horse's silky mane, he sensed that Vitus was every bit as excited as he was; a new life beckoned for both of them.

CHAPTER TWO

The Countess's Bargain

Most people know the famous story of Lady Godiva and her husband Leofric, Earl of Mercia, whose decision to charge extra taxes from the people of Coventry prompted Lady Godiva to ride naked through the streets of the town. It is doubtful whether the story is really true, and some people think that monks in the Middle Ages "embroidered" the story to encourage tourism. It may be that "naked" really meant that she had all her clothes on except for her fine jewellery and furs … but that doesn't capture the imagination so much! In real life, in the eleventh century, she and Leofric certainly did a great deal for Coventry, and the legend of her "naked" ride means that even today, whoever has heard of Coventry has also heard of Lady Godiva.

E dith was truly miserable that April day in Evesham, even though it was her birthday ... 3rd April, 1047, and today she was seven. Some days before, Griffith, her father's wizard, had pronounced it a particularly important day in her life.

As they had sat at table one evening the wizard had said to her father, Wulfric, "You chose, my lord, to name the child Edith, and when our blessed King Edward married a lady called Edith, this was a sign that God smiled on the child. The king's own consecration in Winchester was on the child's third birthday ... little Edith is destined by God to be linked in fortune with kings and queens!"

Wulfric had smiled, perhaps rather indulgently, for these Welsh wizards were always "imaginative" (Wulfric's word for "crazy..."), but he allowed Griffith to go on.

"I advise that Edith be set on a fresh pathway in her life, on her seventh birthday. You will know, my lord, that seven is an especially important magical number?" He paused, so that Wulfric had time to digest this information.

"Edith's birth was on the third day of the fourth month – the numbers here, as you will see, add up to seven. Well, we live in the year 1047. Now, whichever way these numbers are added together, you arrive eventually at the Blessed number of three – Our Lord's number, the number of the Holy Trinity! My lord, a child who reaches the age of seven, in a year whose numbers add up to three, whose birthday is on the third day, whose day and month of birth add up to seven, is truly a blessed child!"

As Griffith sat down, his long grey beard trembling, there was a scattering of applause from his audience, impressed if a little confused by all these threes and sevens.

"What you have said has much of wisdom," Edith's father murmured, "and I shall indeed act on your advice." Edith remembered feeling a slow trickle of fear slip down her spine.

"On her seventh birthday we shall send Edith to the household of one of my dearest friends, in a family much favoured by the king. She shall be taught how to behave appropriately for one so chosen by God, as you say. Our great church of the Holy Trinity here in Evesham ("there's that number three again," thought Edith) was the gift of the beautiful Countess of Mercia, our dear friend the Lady Godiva. Edith shall leave us, to live with her and learn from her example!"

Her father was sending her to Coventry! Edith looked across to her mother, hoping that she would say something to contradict her father, but she saw only a blank face. There would be no help from her...

And indeed there had been none. Wulfric's wife was hardly more than a girl herself, and it had been no good appealing to her. She might well believe that it was a special thing for the family, for her daughter to be singled out and sent to live in the household of one of the most powerful couples in the land – Godiva and her husband the Earl Leofric. So Edith found herself – and on her birthday too! – packed off with two men-servants to keep her company, on the long journey from Evesham to Coventry.

It had been an exceptionally hard winter, so severe that no man living could remember another like it. The trees were still rigid and black against the pale sky, with no hint of welcome leaf. A few thin cattle were seen trying to graze the still rock-hard ground, and Edith's journey was not even lightened by birdsong, as so many creatures had died from cold or hunger. She was filled with dread as her little party approached Coventry from the hillside overlooking it, and as she looked down, all she saw was a small collection of timber houses dotted among the enormous stone buildings belonging, she guessed, to Godiva, her husband Leofric, and to the church. She had been told about the newly-built wonder, St Mary's Priory, a truly huge religious house, which she now saw towering over all the other buildings.

All was quiet at the great house of the Earl Leofric when Edith arrived early that evening. As it was still Lent, a time of meditation before Easter, there was no laughing or shouting to be heard, and even the great bell in the tower above the house had been muffled. Edith was ushered into a small room by a girl of about twelve, she guessed, who was trying hard to suppress her natural high spirits in these long dark days before the feast of Easter-tide. Before she knew it, her bundles of belongings were at her feet, the men-servants had faded into the shadows and gone to stable the horses before their long ride home tomorrow, and the girl was placing more logs on the fire.

Abruptly the door swung open, allowing a shaft of torch-light from the Great Hall beyond to pierce the room with almost dazzling brilliance. In its bright rays stood Leofric's wife, the Lady Godiva.

"So you are Edith!" she cried, and much to Edith's astonishment, half-ran to her and swung her up in the air, placing her on the table. "And how are you, my little one?" Before Edith could recover herself Godiva was talking and talking, of families and pets, of journeys and home-comings, and all the good things they had to look forward to at Easter. How beautiful she is, thought Edith, studying at close range the delicate pink complexion, the blue, blue eyes – prettier than any Edith had ever seen – and especially the marvellous spun-gold hair, twisted into such coils and plaits as one would not think possible. Edith was later to see these plaits braided even more stunningly with tiny jewels and beads, though at present a plainer style was needed, for Lent.

"And today is your birthday!" Godiva exclaimed. She signalled to the servant girl to come over, and Edith noticed for the first time that she was carrying something. "Here is a present from me, to welcome you and to say "Happy Birthday". I hope you will like him." Placed in Edith's arms, as she stood there, still on the table, was the bundle from the girl's arms – a wriggling, snuffling, hound-pup.

"He is a wolf-hound, Edith," said Godiva with a twinkle. "Your father's name is Wulfric – why don't you call him Wulf?"

Edith looked down at the warm little animal, at his huge ungainly paws and his black shiny eyes and nose, and looked across at Godiva with happy tears beginning to sting her eyes.

"Oh yes, I will – thankyou, my lady," she burst out, hugging Wulf close as her tears splashed on his upturned nose. But Godiva had gone, the door was closed, and all Edith remembered of the rest of her birthday was the warm fire, the welcome bed, and Wulf licking her chin as he snuggled next to her tired body.

The months that followed passed like a dream for Edith. She was given the freedom of being treated as a child of the family, and repaid them by behaving well. She was a little afraid of Leofric, it was true, though she saw him only rarely: he was busy not only with affairs of state, since he was one of the king's most trusted advisers, but also with looking after his and Godiva's lands and properties in Coventry and the surrounding area. Only four years before, they had been granted the privilege of founding an abbey – St Mary's Priory – here in the town, and had been given many manors by their grateful, newly-crowned king. The abbey was a vast, wonderful building, and Godiva had taken a particular interest in ornamenting it. There were stories that she had employed goldsmiths and silversmiths to change her jewellery into images and crosses for it!

Although Edith was young, she soon realised that Leofric was not a naturally good man, as Godiva was an instinctively good woman. She heard talk that he had been ambitious as a young man, and had led many battles in his time. He was also shrewd where money was concerned. Edith could see that his one weakness was his wife – and who could blame him, with such a one as Godiva? The people of the town loved and respected her, too, and Godiva could turn the earl's mood from gloom to cheer at the smallest click of her fingers.

Usually. When Edith had been four months in the household, she was playing in the courtyard with Wulf one day when he bounded off after a ball and Edith could not run fast enough to keep up with him. Tired, she went indoors, and as she passed through a passageway she stopped in her tracks upon realising that Leofric and Godiva were in the Great Hall – and were quarrelling. For a moment Edith's heart jumped a beat, as Leofric sounded so angry.

"There is nothing to discuss, Godiva: you need not concern yourself with this business. There may be trouble with the Danes soon and the king will need help. I must tax the people more – after the hard winter, we have used up our household provisions, as you well know, and new supplies of food and fuel are becoming more and more expensive. Corn alone has increased in price six-fold! With such costs I must increase taxes; how else can I keep our household in food and warmth, and my men and horses in good readiness?"

"Fighters and horses!" exclaimed Godiva. "What about the people? Haven't they suffered terribly from this winter, too? They have come to the point of starvation, and have frozen in their poor dwellings with little wood for their fires. How will they be able to survive the next winter if they can afford even less food and fuel? I would give every stitch of clothing from my body to help them, rather than take more taxes to put another log on my fire!"

There was a pause.

"You do that, then, madam. Your generosity is well-known – perhaps too much for our own good. I will make a bargain with you: discard your clothing, as you suggest, and give it to the poor. Show them you care – mount your horse and ride naked through the town. If you do, I will cancel these increases in taxes."

Shocked, Edith crept away.

For some days afterwards a heavy cloak of silence hung around the house. Neither Leofric nor Godiva gave any sign of their disagreement when in public, though Edith noticed Leofric's black eyebrows twitching occasionally as if his troubles were struggling to show themselves on his face. Eleanor, the girl who had met Edith on that first night, seemed thoughtful, too, as she went about her business of tending to Godiva.

A week after the argument, just as dawn was breaking, Edith was roused from sleep by Wulf, whining to be let out of her bed-chamber. He simply couldn't be ignored, and so she stumbled to open the door to the courtyard. What her sleepy eyes saw there made her wake up with a jolt, though she had to pinch herself to make sure she wasn't dreaming.

Wulf had heard horses' hooves, and with a hound's instinct had perhaps been hoping that a hunt might be beginning. But he was disappointed: Leofric had in fact gone hunting after boar the previous night, and was still absent from the house. The horse Wulf had heard wore no hunting tack, not even a saddle, but seated on it was Lady Godiva, equally unadorned. She wore nothing at all – only that wonderful gold hair, now loosened, and falling long and shimmering to cloak her body, covering all but her pale legs. Edith blinked in the morning haze, and Godiva bowed her head gracefully towards her, saying nothing. Eleanor led the horse out under the arched gateway – no men-servants were to be seen – and in no time Edith was left alone at the door, holding a puzzled Wulf.

***

Godiva rode that August morning through every street in the town, with only her hair to cover her nakedness. Eleanor had given away Godiva's finest clothes on the previous night, telling the people as she went, to sell them in exchange for food and fuel. She also told of her mistress's plan for the following morning. Everyone in the town, shocked by the bargain Leofric had struck with his wife, and amazed by Godiva's decision, had promised to remain indoors and out of respect would avoid looking outside until they had heard Godiva's horse go by.

Leofric, meanwhile, had returned after dawn, tired, from his boar-hunt. He had called for Godiva but had found her nowhere. Finally he had come across Edith, who was crying in the doorway, from which she had not moved all morning. When he heard what Edith had seen, Leofric's eyes moistened, and he looked away, rumpling Wulf's ear thoughtfully. Suddenly he bent down and kissed Edith's forehead, before striding towards the chapel, still in his grimy hunting clothes. He remained there, silently praying, until Godiva's return.

CHAPTER THREE

The White Hart

One of the most important moments in English history occurred in Coventry at the end of the fourteenth century. The king, Richard II, was thought to be weak, and other powerful men were challenging his rule. Two in particular, Mowbray and Bolingbroke, were thought to present a danger. The two men were enemies, and had accused each other of treason. The king's uncle, Gloucester, had been murdered, and Bolingbroke accused Mowbray of being involved. Nobody would admit the truth, and after many arguments, Richard decided to set up a "trial by combat" on Gosford Green in Coventry. The idea behind such trials was that whoever won was the innocent one! What happened next – or didn't happen – sealed the king's fate and determined the future of English royalty.

Matthew, fetch me some wine from Mistress Margery's immediately; here lad, take the money."

"Wine, father? But..."

"Yes, wine, lad – we can't celebrate the king's visit by drinking ale like common people; go on, be quick about it."

The king's visit. So it was true. His Majesty King Richard II was bringing his court to Coventry.

Matthew was an eager listener to the grown-ups' conversation at dinner that night. His father was unusually excited, and from time to time brought his fist down so heavily on the table that the plates shook.

"I tell you, brother John, this man Henry Bolingbroke is a danger to our well-being. And as for Thomas Mowbray, the saints preserve us from such a man! The king is right to order them to fight – in trial by combat, whoever is the loser, we're rid of at least one trouble-maker!"

Master Russell gulped down a wedge of rabbit pie with such violence that he had to call for more drink to wash it down. When the commotion of his coughing was over, Uncle John took up the conversation.

"The king is involved in these dark deeds himself, brother. Was Mowbray involved in Gloucester's death? Who knows, but it's my belief Richard knew what was afoot, all right. Bolingbroke has had the courage to accuse Mowbray in open court, and the king must settle his own conscience by letting the two men fight it out. I fear that only bad things will come of these matters; I just wish it hadn't been Coventry chosen for the combat. I hear, by the way, that a great deal of preparation is going on at both of Mowbray's castles, here at Caludon and Brinklow. Bolingbroke is going to stay at Baginton Castle, the home of Sir Walter Bagot. They have both ordered new armour, Mowbray from Milan and Bolingbroke from Germany. Such fine armour means business!"

"The king involved! What nonsense! Gossip that only the servants would believe! Brother, I'll not listen to any more of this...this...treason!"

Master Russell's eyes grew red and large, the veins around them standing out like the blue cloth he dealt in.

"The name of Richard should be blessed in this town! His dear father the Black Prince – may God rest his soul – was a great soldier abroad, yet spent many years helping to create peace and prosperity here. I myself remember the prayers of thanks we gave for his victory at Crécy, when I was just a boy. And you cast doubt upon his son the king?"

Matthew groaned inside: he knew that his father was thinking of the links between Coventry and the royal family and would soon be reciting them all for everyone's benefit: the Black Prince's grandmother, Queen Isabella, had inherited land here and the prince himself had often used Cheylesmore Manor as a hunting lodge. The seal of the city itself bore the motto "Camera Principis" or "the Prince's Chamber", showing its close tie with the Black Prince, and the crest on his armour, a cat-a-mountain, was on the city's coat of arms. He had heard it all before, too many times!

"Enough!" Matthew's mother stood up from the table. "Husband, such matters are none of our concern. I will have no more of your talk, I tell you – and besides, look how the boy listens to you both; a fine example to set. Alice, play us a little music on that lute of yours. We need something to soothe our brains."

Matthew quickly finished his meal and moved to be near the fire while his sister played. That night his dreams were filled with armed knights, the clash of steel and the king himself, watching over everything under the weight of his glittering crown …

***

So a tournament was coming. The next few weeks were full of hurly-burly. Matthew's father, newly-created Master of the great Trinity Guild, and a much-respected draper, had been appointed by his fellow citizens to present the king with Coventry's gift to mark the occasion, once the combat was over. It was to be a great bale of the finest cloth the city was capable of weaving – and in Coventry only the best was good enough. It was dyed in the wondrous deep blue now known throughout the land as "Coventry Blue". King Richard adored fine clothes. His sleeves, Matthew had heard, reached right down to the floor, and were caught up by delicate gold chain fastened with the king's own symbol – a tiny white hart, or stag – serving the purpose of buttons.

Master Russell was bursting with pride at the honour bestowed upon him; he deserved it though, thought Matthew, as there was no more loyal servant of the king. Yet even he, Matthew realised, was disturbed by the king's recent style of government: being fond of clothes and poetry was all very well, but it cost a great deal of money to supply the king with all the luxuries he demanded, money which ought to have been spent on wars. Richard was no soldier-king as his father the Black Prince would have been, if he'd lived to be king himself. Now there were rumours that Richard had been involved in killing his own uncle, the Duke of Gloucester, and was blaming it on others... Nobody knew who was really responsible, and the king was quite happy to allow Bolingbroke to accuse Mowbray. The king disliked them both, and mistrusted them both. If one of them was killed in the combat he would not be sorry. What a tangle it all was.

"Whatever men may say about all that," Master Russell insisted, "Richard is a good friend to Coventry. He has provided money for the city, and stone from his quarries here for carrying on building the great walls. Our great walls will one day surround the fairest city in all England!" he said.

***

That September morning, when Matthew woke, he could already hear the muffled babble of people as they made their way past the house towards Gosford Green, where the tournament was to take place. On the previous day, Matthew had been given the day off from the priory school, and had cart-wheeled and tumbled his way to the Green, where enormous tents were being put in place for the combatants to retire to, and a great dais had been put up, from which the king and his favourites were to view the proceedings.

Already there was an air of festival about the place – there were stalls selling sweetmeats and souvenir tokens, and sucking-pigs were being roasted on great spits. Men were hammering in tent-pegs and stopping to quench their thirsts with huge flagons of ale; wandering players were practising dances and decorating hobby-horse heads with ribbons and bows. Best of all, though, was the sight of the many knights who followed Bolingbroke or Mowbray, who had arrived early to look over the fighting ground, supervise arrangements for the horses and find the best viewpoints from which they and their ladies could watch the combat. Matthew had never seen such sights, and his heart thumped horribly inside him when he remembered that he, Matthew Russell, was to walk alongside his father right up to the king's throne, to kneel at the king's own feet while his father presented the gift.

"The king is fond of children," his father had said, "and you are a fine-looking boy. Who knows, he may decide to take you as a page?"

Matthew was amazed to think of it: to be part of the king's own household, and see the places he had only heard about from travelling salesmen who visited his father; to listen to the court musicians – a far cry from Alice's twanging on the lute!

So, the day had arrived. Matthew scrambled to the tub where he had been told to have an extra-thorough wash, including his curly black hair. His mother had set out his new jerkin and hose, and he was to wear the exquisite shoes which his uncle Percy had made specially at his shoemaker's workshop in Spon Street. When he was dressed, Matthew admired his reflection in the water. Not bad, he thought.

Many hours later, Matthew was seated next to his father and Uncle John in the corner of the huge viewing area at the Green. He was feeling sick, partly because he knew that as soon as the combat was over, and one of the lords lay dead, he would have to cross the arena to present the king's cloth; partly, also, because the day was so hot that there was a horrible smell from the thousands of sweaty bodies all around him.

The two combatants' standards blazed in the sunshine, and their proud horses' armour glinted as they pawed the ground. Bolingbroke could be seen in front of his tent, when suddenly Matthew realised it was all about to begin. He held his breath.

The constable and marshal, who supervised proceedings, approached Bolingbroke and loudly demanded why he had come to the city. Boldly came his reply: "I am Henry of Lancaster, Duke of Hereford. I have come here to do my endeavour against Thomas Mowbray, Duke of Norfolk, as a traitor, untrue to God, the king, his realm and me."

The crowd, who had been buzzing with excitement, fell silent. Matthew saw Bolingbroke unsheath his sword, and swore on it that his quarrel was true and just.

What a sight followed. Here came the king! Accompanied by a great train of all the peers of the realm, he took his seat upon the great dais. Then a proclamation was called, that no man could approach the field of combat on pain of death. Matthew shivered. This was real.

Mowbray was ready, too. Like his opponent, he made his oath before the constable and marshal that his quarrel was just and true and shouted, "God aid him that hath the right!"

It all happened so fast after that: the men were handed their lances. Bolingbroke dropped his visor and as the trumpet sounded his horse reared up and he raced towards Mowbray, who moved quickly forward. But what was happening? Matthew strained his eyes and ears, unable to believe what was going on; a herald had rushed onto the combat ground – the king had thrown down his sceptre!

The crowd roared, then suddenly fell silent. Mowbray and Bolingbroke reined in their horses, and were told to hand back their lances. The king had risen to his feet – a slight, thin-featured man, dignified, thought Matthew, but frail. He looked pale, and was steadying himself by gripping tightly the carved head of a lion which formed the arm-rest of his throne.

"My lords and ladies, and citizens of Coventry," the king began, "today we have come to this place to witness the trial by combat between Henry Bolingbroke, Duke of Hereford, and Thomas Mowbray, Duke of Norfolk. We take no pleasure in this fight, and will shortly decide how to proceed." Unsteadily, he then made his way into the royal tent.

Hours rolled past. Why had the king stopped the fight? Nobody wanted to move from their spot; stall-holders did no business and musicians remained silent. Matthew dared not look at his father and Uncle John. He was simply aware of a quiet buzz from the crowd, anxiously waiting for the king's decision.

When it came, it shocked them all.

"Proceedings are closed!" declared the king's herald. "Bolingbroke, Duke of Hereford, is banished from these shores for a span of ten years, and his estates are forfeit to the king. Mowbray, Duke of Norfolk must prepare himself, on pain of death, for exile from this land … forever."

Both men were summoned to kneel before the king's dais, and swear an oath to agree to the king's decision. They also, so Matthew faintly heard, swore not to continue their argument if they should meet when abroad.

A cold trickle of sweat made its way down Matthew's spine. The sun seemed to burn his eyeballs. He noticed the vein on his father's forehead beginning to pulse alarmingly. The crowd was silent at first, but when the king sat down, people began to shake themselves into believing what had just happened. Could it be so? Was the king really such a fool? Instead of getting rid of one troublemaker, was he really taking the risk of allowing these two powerful men to gather supporters abroad? Neither of them had any time for the other, but now that the king had treated them both so badly, was it not possible that they might join forces and attempt a rebellious return? Even I can see this happening, thought Matthew, and I'm just a Coventry draper's son.

It could only mean one thing: the king was indeed a weakling, who couldn't stand the sight of blood. Uncle John had been right.

That evening Matthew heard angry outbursts from many of the people who were travelling miserably home. It wasn't the disappointment of missing out on a fight; no, it was much more serious. The young king had made a serious miscalculation, and the future looked all the more uncertain because of it.

The king himself had retreated from the field; he would not meet anyone. They had not been allowed to present their gift of Coventry cloth. Master Russell, his moment of glory in ruins and his loyalty to the king sorely tested, had kept a stony silence all the way home. All he had said before shutting himself up in his office, the treasured cloth lying forlorn on the floor, was, "It's a sad blow for Coventry; the Black Prince will tonight lie unquiet in his grave."

Matthew kicked miserably at the pile of logs in front of the fire, scuffing those wonderful shoes he had worn so proudly in the morning. As his father called roughly for wine – "May as well drink it, just the same!" – Matthew had an idea.

***

King Richard was picking fretfully at a pigeon's wing where he dined with the monks of Charterhouse, on the road out of Coventry towards London. He had responded sulkily to their guided tour of the building, which he was seeing for the first time since he had laid its foundation-stone, fourteen years previously. He was thinking longingly of the peacefulness of his orchards back at Eltham Palace, in the south of his realm.

Suddenly a commotion was evident at the tapestry end of the long dining-hall. Monks were whispering urgently and holding back a small figure who was struggling to get free of them …

"What is this?" Richard asked peevishly. "Can the king not dine in peace even in the house of the brethren? What causes this nuisance?"

Matthew – of course, he was the "nuisance" – ran between the monks who were surrounding him, right up to the high table. Shaking with fear, tiredness and a kind of feverish excitement, he thrust onto the table the bale of cloth which his father had dumped in the office at home. Dishes on the table jumped and whirled, making some of the sauces in them spill over.

"My lord," Matthew remembered himself at last, and fell to his knees. "I mean, Your Majesty, I would like to present with the compliments of the city of Coventry and the great Trinity Guild, this ..." A monk caught hold of his arm, almost ripping his jerkin as he tried to pull away this impertinent boy.

"No, stay," ordered the king. "Let him go on." He leaned curiously across the table and touched the fine cloth admiringly. "Why have you, boy, brought this to me now? Where have you come from, with your clothes all spattered with mud?"

Matthew was aware of men springing up to protect the king, though he hardly looked a threat. He looked down at himself. It was true: his clothes were speckled with clay from the roads, his beloved shoes almost falling apart. He wiped the sweat from his forehead with the back of his hand, leaving a smear from hairline to eyebrow. Richard smiled unexpectedly.

"My father is the master draper of the city, sire," he began, "and was to have given you this cloth as a measure of our esteem and loyalty this afternoon, but ... but you would receive no-one, after you had ..." his voice faded away.

"Go on," said the king.

"No man in this city loves you more than my father, Your Majesty. It was to have been the golden moment of his life – yet even he says that you were wrong today; he is bitterly disappointed. I wanted to bring you the present all the same; I have had new clothes made specially for today ..." he broke off, tearfully.

Richard turned to a man who sat, looking pale, beside him.

"So the king is to be criticised by a provincial tradesman, eh? The king is wrong, says the master draper of Coventry." Those in the hall glanced nervously at each other. He paused, and gave a small smile.

"Master draper's son, I have nothing with which to return thanks for your fine gift. Unless you will take this." He reached towards his left wrist, with the long slender fingers of his right hand. "Will this do?"

Matthew caught the small white token as it spun across the table – the white hart button, Richard's own royal symbol.

"Now go," Richard said sharply. "You may convey the thanks of this "wrong" king to your father."

As Matthew backed away from the table, ushered away by the shocked monks, his last sight of King Richard was of a young man holding a narrow band of gold – his crown; he had taken it from his head, and was weighing it thoughtfully in those slender white hands.

***

The exile of Henry Bolingbroke, Duke of Hereford, after the duel in Coventry would change the course of history. Any loyalty he had felt to King Richard II had disappeared, and the final straw came in 1399 when his father John of Gaunt died and Richard confiscated the estates Henry should have inherited.

In June that year, while Richard was campaigning in Ireland, Henry landed in England with an army and claimed the throne. Richard returned in August only to find that powerful forces now supported Bolingbroke; he was made to give up his crown, and Henry now became King Henry IV.

Richard's last journey through Coventry and Warwickshire was as a prisoner. He was imprisoned in Pontefract Castle where in 1400 he died. Some believe he was allowed to starve to death, others that he was murdered on the orders of Henry, the man he had exiled at Coventry on that September day only one year before.

CHAPTER FOUR

Out-Heroding Herod

King Herod was known for his rages, and so Shakespeare described someone who over-acted as "Out-Heroding Herod"

Throughout the Middle Ages some of the first plays in the English language were created and performed by skilled craftsmen (drapers, dyers, tailors, haberdashers and tailors among others) in the most important English towns such as Coventry, Chester and York. They were known as "Mystery plays", not because there was anything mysterious about them, but because "mystere" is French for craft or skill. As, in early days, the Bible was only in Latin, they were a good way of telling people the main stories of the Christian faith.

Coventry's plays were known to have been performed from the fourteenth to the late sixteenth century. They were usually performed at the feast of Corpus Christi, which was at midsummer. Each guild performed on a pageant-wagon, which was a bit like a carnival float, and which was moved from place to place in the city. The Coventry "Herod" was famous: he appeared in the story of how Jesus, Mary and Joseph escaped the order that all new-born male babies should be killed (a story called "The Massacre of the Innocents"). William Shakespeare himself is thought to have travelled from Stratford to see the plays in Coventry … who knows whether they inspired him to write his own plays?

As brothers go, Margaret thought, hers wasn't too bad. She and Nicholas actually got on very well as a rule, although as he was nearly two years older than her, he did order her about rather a lot. At the moment, though, Margaret was really fed up with him. "Conceited pig," she said to herself. "Just because he's got a big part in the play and I've only got a few words to say, there's no need to keep on and on about it. I'll be glad when it's all over."

Secretly Margaret was really proud of Nicholas, though she would never own up to it. While she, along with many of her friends, was playing an angel (unlikely casting, her mother said!) Nicholas was to be the messenger to Herod's court. You might not think that this is very important, but to Nicholas it was very special: he would be on stage at the same time as Master Richardson, famous for being the best Herod in the country. He was so good that travellers and merchants from all the other great cities of England said that no-one played the part so well anywhere else. Only last year a man from York had said, "This Herod will go down in history; ours is a timid fellow compared to this monster." It was true that Richardson, a master tailor, was frightening: he was a champion wrestler and a man of very quick temper, as Nicholas his apprentice had often discovered. Richardson's temper came in handy in his acting of Herod, as he considered him a wicked tyrant who should be shown as a savage, evil man.

Margaret was now absolutely sick of hearing about the play. For weeks she had been listening to Nicholas say his lines, and hearing her mother showing off to her friends about Nick's good fortune. Her brother had an excellent memory, and was always giving complete performances of the play while the family sat at dinner, putting on all the different voices of the players. His voice had recently broken to a more gruff tone, and the family loved his squeaky imitations of the Angel Gabriel.

***

"Come on, Margaret, do try to look a little more enthusiastic, dear," said her mother as she woke her up that morning. "It looks like being a fine day. The Watch have been round some time ago unlocking the city gates. You don't want to be late, do you?"

Margaret rubbed the sleep from her eyes wearily and sat up in bed. Her father would by now be telling everyone how, when he was a lad, he played the part of the messenger, in the presence of King Henry VIII and his queen, no less. She had heard it all so many times before. On second thoughts, maybe Father wouldn't bring out the old story today, since it was rumoured that King Henry VIII was now tired of his Queen Katherine, and was keen to be married again, to a beautiful lady called Anne; perhaps it was better for Father to keep quiet.

Sunrise was due at around five o'clock and it was now half an hour before that time. The sight which met Margaret and Nicholas as they left the house was a splendid one. Outside Coventry's St. Nicholas' Church, where the procession was due to begin, hundreds of torch-bearers were waiting for everyone to arrive, the flames lighting up the sky like huge dragon-flies. Eventually everyone was ready to move off on the long walk – first the torch-bearers, guildsmen and their workers, then the children bearing candles before the Corpus Christi or "Body of Christ" itself, this symbol being carried under canopies of silk and cloth of gold, accompanied by the processional crucifix and chalice. Last of all came the priests, monks and nuns of the many religious houses scattered around Coventry. It was a tiring yet emotional occasion, with everyone walking or riding in complete silence except for the chanting of the monks.

It took a long time to reach the other side of town, but as the sun rose, making the torches almost unnecessary as they reached Much Park Street, there was an excitement in the atmosphere that promised a full and memorable day to come. Margaret's eyes slid across to Master Richardson, riding already dressed as Herod, complete with painted leather face-mask and gold and silver crested helmet. This was another honour granted in return for the man's famous acting, since everyone else was still wearing their own best clothes. The blue satin gown looked wonderful, and Richardson sat upon his horse like a king; people nodded their heads in his direction as if to say, "Can't wait – he looks as if he's ready for a fine performance today."

The pageant-wagon – the moveable stage – was drawn out of its "pageant-house" in Mill Lane and all the players stood back and looked at it silently for a few moments, highly satisfied with themselves. Beneath all its splendour it was just a four-wheeled wagon, but today it was … a theatre! Painted cloth hung down on all four sides from the platform, covering the wheels, and underneath was the place where the actors would change, or wait for their entrance. At each of the four corners rose a pole supporting a huge painted canopy, and gaily-coloured banners streamed at the sides. The "stage" floor was strewn with sweet-smelling rushes, and kept underneath were the props as well as the costumes. There were ropes by means of which the whole thing was pulled from one street to another. During the day each craft company would act out its own part of the story, from the Creation of Adam and Eve onwards, until a kind of Bible history had unfolded before the audience's eyes. They would start in Gosford Street, then move on, usually to Much Park Street and on through the city until everyone had seen each of the plays brought to them on the wagons — the audience didn't have to move at all: the theatre came to them! Margaret and Nicholas had cousins acting in the Noah's Ark play. Their own, about the Birth of Jesus and the escape into Egypt, came about halfway along the list.

Nicholas was already jumping up and down in excitement, receiving news from fellow apprentices that other wagons didn't look nearly so impressive, though the Hell's Mouth one, done by the company of cooks, took some beating.

"Not feeling nervous, are you?" a voice spoke suddenly behind Nicholas, coming from behind the fearsome mask and helmet of Master Richardson.

"Oh … no sir," replied Nicholas. "I just can't wait to start!"

"I don't think you'll have to wait long now, they're giving the signal to move off. We'll be at the playing-place in Gosford Street in about a quarter of an hour. Be sure to remember your lines – and fasten that belt a bit more tightly, lad – you look sloppy!"

"Yes sir, sorry sir," replied Nicholas now feeling really nervous, especially because he knew that Margaret was listening. "Oh and good luck, Master Richardson!"

Richardson, who had been walking away, turned round abruptly and everyone in earshot could hear the anger in his voice. "You *idiot* boy, he hissed, "Don't you know anything? Never wish an actor good luck – it's *bad* luck!"

Margaret could not resist it. "You *idiot* boy!" she mimicked once Richardson had gone away. "I thought everyone knew that you're supposed to say "break a leg" to wish an actor good luck. Some actor you are!"

Miserably Nicholas fastened his belt. "Damn, damn, *damn*," he muttered.

By three o'clock that afternoon their play had been performed many times. Margaret's angelic songs had been a success and she was enjoying herself, even admitting that Nicholas was acting pretty well. Herod, of course, was as wonderful as ever, and the crowds were loving it, especially when he jumped down from the wagon and rampaged angrily amongst the audience, roaring with fury at the news that Mary and Joseph had fled with Jesus. No other Herod in the land ever got down from the wagon to act, and the Coventry crowds loved the extra drama of him pushing and shoving people in every direction.

They were about to set up for a performance in Cross Cheaping when Nicholas, white-faced, appeared at Margaret's side.

"Something terrible's happened! It's all going to be ruined! It's all my fault, for wishing him luck! We'll be the laughing stock of the city! It's a disaster!"

"What are you talking about? What's happened, for goodness' sake?" snapped Margaret.

"It's Herod – I mean Richardson," he replied." He's lost his voice! Not only that, but when he jumped off the wagon in Jordan Well he twisted his ankle. What are we going to do? He won't perform if he can't do it perfectly, and he can hardly speak. And if he won't perform, none of us can … maybe the crowd will throw things at the wagon!"

"I'm surprised you don't play it yourself then. Your voice is breaking and you know all the lines," said Margaret sarcastically. "I've had to listen to you often enough."

Nicholas went quiet.

"Do you know, I think I could! No-one would know it was me under the mask!"

"Oh you're so right," said Margaret sarcastically. "Master Richardson's only the best Herod in England. He should be really easy to replace, especially since the replacement is the brilliant, the one and only Nicholas Corbett!"

"But I *could* do it, Margaret!" Nicholas shouted, jumping up." I know I could. There's only one thing – you'd have to play my part of the messenger."

"Nicholas … it would be obvious I'm a girl."

"No it wouldn't," Nicholas insisted." Because we look very alike, and you're not much smaller than me. You know my part because we've rehearsed together. It isn't a very *big* part, anyway."

"You'd never think it," thought Margaret privately. Aloud, she surprised herself by saying "All right – I'll do it, on condition that no-one knows but us two and Master Richardson."

"I won't forget this, sis," beamed Nick. And neither of them did …

***

Margaret finished her opening speech quickly, and pointed to the corner of the wagon, where Nicholas was to stride forward as Herod. She had remembered to shout her words very loudly, as heralds should.

Nicholas had begun his boastful speech, announcing how wonderful he was.*

> *"The mightiest conqueror that ever walked ground*
> *For I am even he that made heaven and hell*
> *And of my mighty power hold up the world so round..."*

He sounded very much like Richardson, thought Margaret; he seemed to have the knack of impersonating other voices, and the mask disguised his true voice even further.

> *"When they come again, they shall die that same day!"*

Margaret could hardly contain a smile as Nicholas paced up and down the stage, brandishing a big stick, glaring down at the audience and frightening a few children, who clung to their mothers.

"I rant, I rave, and now I run mad!" continued Nicholas, and with that he jumped off the wagon and pushed his way through the crowds, throwing people off-balance all about him and recklessly waving his stick around. Letting out wild roars of rage he shoved his way through knots of spectators, before leaping back onto the wagon and hissing through his teeth,

> *"All young children for this shall be dead,*
> *With sword to be slain ..."*

Furious that baby Jesus had escaped his clutches, Herod was now planning to kill *all* new-born children.

The crowd went suddenly quiet, absorbing the horror of what he had said, and Margaret felt that many women in the audience hugged their children a little more tightly. But Nicholas had a bit more raging to do yet! When one of his soldiers, obviously unwilling to kill babies, suggested that such a plan would cause an uprising, Nicholas cried,

---

* *The play's quotations are from the play of the Coventry Shearmen and Tailors.*

"A rising? Out! Out! Out!" and he leapt off the wagon again and brandished the soldier's sword. This was great stuff – even Richardson hadn't jumped off the wagon *twice*. Not surprisingly the soldiers agreed to "slaughter the innocents" and very soon Mary and Joseph were escaping to Egypt and the most moving part of the play began. The mothers walked on, slowly singing what was later to be known all over the world as the lovely "Coventry Carol", a sad, mournful lullaby to the children who were about to be murdered upon Herod's orders.

"Lullay, lullay, my little tiny child,
By by lully lullay.."

Nicholas was breathing lightly; Margaret could sense his satisfaction that the play was coming to its end, the Holy Family had escaped, and all had gone well.

"Herod King, I shall thee tell
All thy deeds are come to nought."

It was then that Nicholas made another change to the drama. In the script Herod was supposed to say, *"Saddle my horse, for in haste I will go. After these traitors I now will ride"* and then he and all the other actors usually took their bows before the wagon was pulled on to the next playing-place. Nicholas, however, shouted these words and to everyone's astonishment, vaulted from the stage onto the back of one of the knight's horses, threw the rider off, dug his heels into the horse's flanks and charged his way through the startled crowds!

At first the audience was too surprised to applaud, but soon burst out cheering, clapping and stamping, calling for the return of "Master Richardson". Nicholas wheeled the horse round and cantered back, to share the applause with his fellow actors and give an apologetic slap on the back to the knight whose horse he'd taken. Beneath the stage, behind the curtains, the real Richardson heard the tumultuous applause and sighed to himself. Was this the end of his day playing Herod? The lad had been brilliant. It was hard to swallow, but he would have to hand the part over in future.

Meanwhile Margaret and Nicholas were rushing on to the next playing-place, near St. John's Church. Amongst all the other congratulations, Margaret smiled secretly at her brother, whose mask still covered his face. Suddenly their mother appeared at their side, very excited and proud.

Boldly shaking Nicholas' hand she said, "Well, Master Richardson, you were *excellent* – but don't you think my Nicholas was good too? You couldn't have chosen better for your messenger – Nicholas my boy, well done!" And with that she planted a huge wet kiss on Margaret's painted face, remarking casually, "Heaven knows where your sister's got to – probably still sulking, eh?"

Margaret avoided looking at Nicholas, who was trying hard not to laugh. "Yes, mother," she replied dutifully. "She probably still is."

CHAPTER FIVE

The Queen at the Inn

During the reign of Queen Elizabeth I (1558-1603) there was great anxiety about who should succeed her to the throne. She did not marry or have children, and the nearest heir to the throne of England was her cousin, Mary, Queen of Scots. Not only did Elizabeth dislike her, there was also the question of Mary's religion: she was a Catholic. In previous years, during the reign of Elizabeth's sister, Queen Mary I, who was herself a Catholic, there had been terrible persecution of Protestant believers. Mary herself became known as "Bloody Mary". Protestant men had been burnt at the stake in Coventry, and no-one wanted the "bad old days" of Catholicism to return.

Queen Elizabeth attempted to keep the peace between religious factions, but was alarmed when rebellion broke out in the north in November 1569, as the rebels seemed to back Mary Queen of Scots as a successor to Elizabeth. Elizabeth had already imprisoned Mary at Tutbury, near Burton on Trent, and now the Catholic Queen was moved south for greater security – to Coventry. She was first moved to the Bull Inn in Smithford Street, and then to St Mary's Hall. In early January 1570 she was sent back to Tutbury.

I t was a late November morning, bleak with heavy mists, and a penetrating cold struck upwards from the ground. It felt as if the watery sun peeping from behind the clouds was crying for the sad young queen, who rode surrounded by guards.

Mary, the Catholic Queen. She was only 27 years old when she came to Coventry, but her life had been so filled with trouble that she seemed much older. Now, after enduring imprisonment in Tutbury in Staffordshire for so long, she was being sent even farther away from her beloved Scotland and at an even safer distance from the latest rebellion in the north of England. The rebels, it seemed, wanted to place the Catholic Queen on the throne of both Scotland and England. Coventry was a good choice of prison, thought England's Queen Elizabeth, in which to hide away this troublesome cousin of hers. It was not too close to London, and it was a good long way from Scotland. Even better, it was a town which hated Catholics, and so Mary was likely to have an uncomfortable time of it.

Queen Elizabeth was right about the Catholic-hating citizens of Coventry. The day before Mary rode in silence through the fortress-like walls of the city there had been quite a rumpus at the Bull Inn there. Thomas and Anne Hillyer, twin children of the landlord and his wife, had overheard a terrible argument between their parents. At sunset a loud knocking had been heard at the yard door, and the boy-messenger who had been making such a noise had come from the Mayor's Parlour. He said that the Mayor was being ordered to find lodgings for the treacherous Scottish queen and her guards, and he had decided on the Bull Inn. Landlord Hillyer, however, took a different view.

"The Mayor can sleep in the streets himself, and give *his* bed to the scheming woman, but I'll not have her here in *my* house. Is he trying to put me out of business? What will happen to my trade, if people hear I have a Catholic under my roof?"

"Please listen, Master Hillyer," replied the boy nervously. "It's only for a short time. He only asks for your help for a few days – a week, perhaps."

"A WEEK?" stormed Hillyer. "Are you laughing at me, boy? That woman will not stay in my house an *hour*, and that's final!"

At this point Thomas and Anne's mother spoke up. She was a sensible woman with a keen, practical common sense.

"What nonsense, William – you really think customers will stay away because of a Scottish girl? Why, they'll flock here; she's meant to be a good-looking lassie, you know! And what about her guards? They'll be mighty pleased to stay in an inn, and the bill for their ale will come to a pretty penny – all reclaimable from the Mayor. You can't turn down business in *November*!"

Thomas and Anne watched their father closely, and felt that they could hear his thoughts going round in his head. He was a proud man, and a stubborn one, but most important of all, an unforgiving one. And he, like many other Coventry people, would not easily forget that only recently, in the reign of Mary Tudor, the present Queen Elizabeth's sister, there had been terrible sights in Coventry. In 1555 – just before the twins were born – three men were burnt at the stake in the city, for keeping to the Protestant faith. Mary Tudor had been a fervent Catholic, and such burnings were a frequent event throughout the country, as she tried to convert the land back to what she called "the true faith". Hillyer had known one of the men, Saunders, well, and respected him highly as a man of principle. He had vowed, on the day of Saunders' gruesome death, that when this queen was dead and replaced by her Protestant sister Elizabeth, he would never have anything to do with any Catholic – man, woman or child. And now he was being asked to give shelter to one, in his own house!

Yet Hillyer could see the sound business sense of his wife, and trade was very bad. There was wisdom in her words.

"But they say she's a witch!" he shouted. "A woman who has murdered and robbed, and left behind her only child in Scotland – she's unnatural! I don't want her here!" Then, looking at the set expression on his wife's face and the despairing features of the messenger, he sat down heavily and said quietly, "Oh, very well. Three nights only, and then she can go to Hell. And after that, if anyone mentions the name of Mary, Queen of Scots in my house, *they* can go to Hell too! Why doesn't the Queen just throw her in the Tower and be done with it?"

Thomas, Anne and the messenger all made a rush for the door, and within minutes the news was spread that the Bull Inn's latest guest would be the Scottish queen-prisoner, her jailer the Earl of Huntingdon and a dozen guards.

Six short weeks later, Thomas was looking back on the day Mary arrived. "Marie" she had said, with a delightfully different accent from any other Thomas had ever heard: Scots, he was told, with some French mixed in. "Mary is such a dull, English name. No, boy, I have lived in France, you know – my name is *Marie*," and she pronounced it with emphasis on the "ee" sound.

That November morning, when she had travelled so sadly into Coventry, was to be a fateful day for the Hillyer family. After the blusterings of the landlord on the previous evening, Mary's reception at the Bull had been a quiet affair. But several hours later, when Thomas and Anne had been getting under the feet of the Earl of Huntingdon's men, Mistress Hillyer had suggested that they go up to the queen's room – "Perhaps a pair of clowns like you two will cheer the lady up," she said. The guards could see no harm in it, and excitedly Thomas and Anne bounded up the stairs.

Neither of them could have put into words what they found so fascinating about Mary: they had certainly seen more beautiful women, but Mary had such a dignified, quiet air about her, which gave off a sort of calm – so different from their own mother! And when something excited or amused her, her clear grey eyes would sparkle and flash so that her whole face looked much younger. Anne said that the queen's expression reminded her of a cat – the eyes looked thoughtful, watchful, but at times lit up with sparks of fire.

The Queen of Scots had been sitting looking out of the window when she called Thomas and Anne in, and as she turned, put on a polite but tired expression.

"W-we came to see you," said Anne, rather foolishly. "Our mother thought we might cheer you up."

Mary gave a long sigh. "How very kind of your mother – and how do you propose to do that?"

Thomas and Anne both blushed, in embarrassed silence. The Queen realised straight away how thoughtless and rude she had been, and stood up.

"I'm sorry – I really am," she said. "It's a long time since I spoke to children, and for an even longer time I've been imprisoned in one damp, dark place after another. It will take a lot to cheer me up!" And then she smiled, and said, "Well, let's try, shall we?"

When Mistress Hillyer brought the Queen of Scots' meal up to her room, Thomas and Anne had been chattering away there for over two hours. The scene which met the landlord's wife was an astonishing one: the sad-looking woman who had wearily climbed the stairs that very morning was curled up on the floor playing chequers. Not only that, but she had removed her formal gown and was wearing a girlish silk-embroidered dressing-gown, over which her wispy fair-to-red hair tumbled free. She was laughing as she ruffled Thomas' black curly hair, and he was trying to fend her off by clutching at her wrist and dodging under her arm. The tragic face of this morning was transformed into that of a carefree girl.

Before Mistress Hillyer could exclaim at the casual, disrespectful way her children were behaving in the presence of a queen (even if she was a Catholic one), Mary had straightened up, and pushing back her hair, said, "Oh, forgive me Mistress Hillyer! I have kept your children to myself all morning and away from their books. We have had such fun!"

"Mother, please may we come and see the Queen again?" Thomas begged as their mother ushered them out of the room.

"We shall have to see about that," she replied. "Your father doesn't know you've been here at all, and Heaven help you both if he finds out.

Now come; the lady (she refused to call her "the Queen", as Thomas had done) is tired; I will make no promises."

Of course, the children *did* return to the Queen's room – Mary herself had insisted on it. Then, some time later, the order came that she was to be moved on again, to a tiny room high above the Guildhall of St Mary, which was much more like a prison than the Bull Inn. Apparently the landlord's words about "sending Mary to the Tower" had given the Mayor an idea, and he had got some men to clear out the jumble it had contained for many years. Thomas and Anne were horrified to hear the news, and so, it seemed, was the Queen of Scots, who gloomily predicted – correctly – that it would be another damp room to make her rheumatism worse. The move was made, however, and for Mary's safety it was probably just as well.

News had earlier spread that the Catholic Queen was staying at the inn, and as feared, (or welcomed by the landlord) the citizens of Coventry came to drink until all hours, and then had to be forcibly restrained from climbing the stairs to shout abuse at her. Instead, they contented themselves with yelling at her window from the street below, with the night-watchmen of the city happy to do nothing about it. They shouted about her men-friends and her "husband-killing"; her friendship with the old enemies of England, the French; her Catholicism, above all. It didn't matter that gossip had little to do with hard facts: Queen Elizabeth's propaganda machine was all-powerful. The people, Elizabeth's advisers said, must be encouraged to believe that the Scottish Queen was thoroughly *bad*, so that Elizabeth, thoroughly *good*, could feel safe on the throne of England.

Only respect for Master Hillyer stopped the mob from throwing more than abuse at Mary's window while she was at the inn, but they were less worried about it once she was in the guildhall, and many a stone was thrown from the street. And this was not Mary's only discomfort, as the room struck cold, and chill draughts knifed their way through gaps in the stonework, that cold winter. Regular groups of citizens braved the cold to chant anti-Catholic slogans beneath her window, and local preachers thundered from their pulpits about the evil ways of the Scottish Queen. Mary sometimes thought that only one thing kept her from going mad, and that was the visits of Thomas and Anne.

Their mother had agreed that they could visit every day – that glimpse of the game of chequers had touched her deeply – and Huntingdon and his men had no objection. The twins' father would have gone mad at the idea, and so was kept in the dark. The only problem was getting in and out without being seen. Eventually they found a way up through the kitchens, and none but the guards ever knew.

There had been lots to talk about with "Marie": *she* kept *them* entertained, now, with stories about her happy days in France when she was a child, and the time she spent with François, her boy-husband who died before he could become King of France. She told them of her return to Scotland to be its queen, and her fear of the rough Scots men there, who ordered her about. In their turn, Thomas and Anne talked of the games they played, of school, and friends and relatives – anything they could think of, really. It was a happy time for all three.

But during the Christmas period, Mary grew gloomy. Anne thought that this was pretty understandable: whilst she and Thomas talked about the presents they had asked for – and received – Mary was thinking about her own little boy, James. He was now just four and a half, and was being looked after by Protestant "uncles" until he was old enough to become king of Scotland himself – and maybe even England too, said Mary, once. The Queen did not disguise how she disliked these "uncles", who were really only interested in power for themselves, but she knew very little about how her son's mind was being poisoned by Protestants against his Catholic mother. For Mary, being parted from her son was just another instrument of torture being used on her by Elizabeth – the childless Queen of England.

One day in late December, Thomas was boasting as usual about the brilliant pony his father had bought him for Christmas. Anne and the Queen were growing fairly tired of hearing about this marvellous creature. Suddenly, Mary stopped pacing about the room – it was the only exercise she could get, she who had loved all sport, and riding in particular. That was it! James should have a pony as a New Year gift – surely it was possible?

"Where did your father obtain your pony, Thomas?" she asked sharply, cutting into his chatter.

"From my Uncle Edward in Dunchurch – I *told* you!" Thomas said irritably. Fortunately they were now familiar enough with Mary to get away with such rudeness.

"Has he more?"

"Yes, about a dozen more, but some are still too little for *me* to ride," replied Thomas.

"Excellent! Would your uncle sell me a pony for my son, do you think? And could we get the pony to Scotland?"

What a mad scheme it had seemed. Firstly, their uncle was a Catholic-hater. Secondly, would the very act of asking, reveal to their father that they'd been visiting the Queen? Thirdly, how could the pony go to *Scotland*? As far as Thomas was concerned, it was like going to the edge of the world.

The twins reckoned without their mother, however. When Mary herself spoke of the idea to Mistress Hillyer, she was sympathetic. Perhaps she imagined how terrible it would have been to have been separated from her children in the way Mary was suffering now. At any rate, a story was invented that a pony was wanted for a son of one of the guards, and a sturdy little pony, well capable of the journey, had been selected. The price Mary had paid for the animal was more than enough to satisfy Uncle Edward, and he had offered to allow his son Jack to take it to Scotland, with a servant. And then the exciting part … Thomas was to go, too!

Thomas could not believe his luck. Mary's wish was that Thomas, swearing the others to secrecy once they were well away from

Coventry, would tell them the real destination of the pony. Thomas himself was to deliver a letter, in which she wrote to young James, "Remember that in me you have a loving mother." Anne, of course, was madly jealous, especially when their father, not knowing the true story, had said it was all right for Thomas to go as it would "broaden the lad's mind". As if *girls* didn't need their minds broadening! Still, it was a small compensation when Mary said that she couldn't bear to part with both twins at once …

***

It was now another cold morning, with another watery sun, this time a January morning, with icicles hanging stiffly from the thatched roofs as Thomas returned home. "So much for mind-broadening," he thought sullenly. And for the thousandth time since day-break he asked himself the question, "How can I tell her?"

He had bad news for Mary. He did not know that at that very moment she was being moved on yet again, this time back north to be under the guard of the Earl of Shrewsbury and his wife Bess, and that he need not worry about giving his difficult message, as he would never see his Scottish Queen again.

Thomas and the others had travelled as far as Carlisle, near the Scottish border, with Mary's pony. They were stabling their horses at an inn for the night when they were suddenly approached by a rough-looking group of soldiers. The men had wanted to know their business, but they seemed so threatening that Thomas had the horrible feeling that they already knew what it was. Finally they searched them, there and then in the stables.

"Ha!" cried the first of them. "I don't think we need to look much further, lads." He pulled out a letter from Thomas's satchel. Rather surprisingly, he motioned the other soldiers to leave, leading away the precious pony with its gleaming saddle. Thomas began to tremble as he saw the man open the letter's seal, revealing the signature MARIE, as Mary always signed herself, in capital letters. Would they all be hanged, drawn and quartered now, as traitors?

"Go back to your mothers, boys!" the man said quietly. "And don't try any more little favours where Catholics are concerned. You're lucky to escape with your lives. Queen Elizabeth has known about this scheme of yours for some time – she has spies everywhere, you know. She would never allow her cousin Mary to contact her son – that would spell trouble, right enough! Your "Marie" is just a dirty Catholic, anyway, not fit to do anything but scrub floors! Why did you bother to do her a favour when she was just trying to cheat our own Queen?"

"She's no such thing and you …" Thomas began angrily, but Jack sharply punched him in the stomach, which brought him to his senses. The soldier suddenly looked very dangerous.

"Go *home*, little boy, and keep your stupid ideas about Catholics to yourself, if you want to live to be an old man. There'll come a day when any friend of the Catholic Queen will be a dead man – and *she'll* not be allowed to die peacefully in her bed, either. Not if I know Good Queen Bess!"

He turned and followed the rest of the men out onto the high road, and the boys were left to recover. Thomas was violently sick into the straw.

Now, on the homeward trail, Thomas was thinking bitterly about an England which could call its queen "Good" and yet allow her to take away an innocent little boy's present from his own mother

"It would serve old Bess right," he thought, "if James *does* become king of England as well as Scotland, when he grows up!" *

* *Of course, he did – he became King James VI of Scotland and King James I of England in 1603, after Queen Elizabeth's death.*

CHAPTER SIX

A Grim Warning

In the eighteenth and nineteenth centuries capital punishment was legal in England, and it is shocking to realise that hangings regularly took place in Coventry, sometimes for what would now be regarded as minor crimes, as well as for murder. The population accepted the fact, whereas now we regard it as barbaric. In fact, public executions were seen as a kind of entertainment, and crowds of many thousands were common – sometimes as many as 20,000 would be present to witness a hanging. In the Spring of 1765 a notorious hanging took place at the top of what is now the Kenilworth Road, at a place which then became known as Gibbet Hill. It has kept the name to this day. At that time it was in the parish of Stoneleigh and was known as Stoneleigh Common; today it is part of Coventry.

Dan, Dan, Quick! Come here! See what I've found!" William's face appeared round the door. He looked as if he'd seen a ghost. His mad spaniel, Jess, was yapping at his heels and turning circles around them both.

"What now?" Dan asked. His best friend, William, was always picking up items he'd found in the fields, things people had dropped on their way home from market – things he might be able to sell, later on, or if not, bits and pieces they could use in the den they played in together.

He stared at what William held out to him. It was part of a pistol. It still had its flint, and a broken bit of ramrod – it was clearly a soldier's weapon.

"Mam told me about the attack last night," he blurted out. "Did you hear? There was a fight and some men were beaten up. They had lots of money stolen …" Dan stared. He guessed that William had gone looking for stolen money which might have been dropped in the grass. "Anyway," William went on, "one of the men got away and turned up at Mam's friend's house. It was really late, and in the dark she didn't want to let him in until she saw how badly hurt he was. He was bleeding something awful, and by the time she got him in the house he could hardly talk. He's still there, and looks likely to die!" A great shudder took over William's body as he paused for breath.

"Slow down!" Dan cried. "What happened? And how did you get hold of this? What are you going to do with it?"

Gradually William told Dan the story, as his mother had relayed it to the family that morning. Her friend had been "full of it" as she had said. The day before, market day in Coventry, a farmer called Mr Thomas Edwards, from the nearby village of Stoneleigh, had come into town with one of his farm labourers, and they had later spent a lot of time, as market-visitors usually did, in the pub. They had met up with a third man and didn't leave for home until nearly midnight, when they had crossed the fields near the Allesley road. Mr Edwards was a man who could hold his drink, and said he hadn't had much anyway; the others were very much the worse for wear. According to what Mr

Edwards had been able to say before he collapsed, they had been attacked and robbed in the dark, but he presumed the other two had been able to run away. He had been left on his own, at any rate. He was too badly beaten to move at first, but at first light had managed to crawl a distance and raise the alarm.

When his mother had finished the story, William had left the house to search for any clues to what had happened. To his amazement, Jess, with a spaniel's instincts, had quickly found a blood-stained piece of cloth in the field not far from his house. That was when he had come across the pistol, or part of it.

"Right," Dan said. "We have to go to Mr Hewitt."

William went even paler than before. Alderman Hewitt, the Justice of the Peace in Coventry, was a pretty scary man. He had been mayor three times, but more than that was respected – and feared – for his reputation as a "thief-taker". If you were a burglar, a highway robber or any other sort of criminal, Hewitt would be the man to bring you to justice. If anyone could solve a crime, it was him.

Everything happened really quickly after that. Alderman Hewitt confirmed that the pistol was a military one, and was aware that some Dragoons had been based in the city, though they had just left for Warwick. He suspected that, as soldiers do, they might have been hanging round the pubs on the night in question. If Thomas Edwards had been selling goods at market they might have supposed he would have money on him. He thanked the boys, who scuttled back home feeling a mixture of fear and importance.

Later on, Mr Hewitt managed to interview the two men who had run away after being attacked, and they agreed that their attackers were soldiers. As he had thought, he was on the right track, and decided to visit the barracks in Warwick.

Then Thomas Edwards died. Just as William had said, he had been beaten so badly that he didn't recover from his injuries. It was now a murder case! The town was shocked to hear, too, that his poor wife was expecting their sixth child.

A few days later, William was back at Daniel's house.

"They've got them! Last night near us! It was a real ruckus! I saw it all!"

"All right, all right," Daniel said. Will was fit to burst. "Spit it out."

"Well, we heard shouts and bangs down the end of our street, and when we looked out we saw old man Hewitt with a load of others, breaking down the door at the Bakers house."

"What, Moses Baker?" asked Daniel. His father knew him well – like most people in the district, Moses was a ribbon weaver.

"Yes, him," William continued impatiently. "It was not long after midnight, and they pulled him out of the house. He was shouting and trying to fight them off, but he could see it was useless. Mam says he's confessed to the murder, along with the two soldiers!"

And so the story unfolded. Moses Baker, "a wrong'un if ever I saw one," Daniel's dad said, had joined up with two soldiers who had been staying at the Red Lion near his house, and they had gone looking for someone to rob. Alderman Hewitt had the two men arrested. They were called Edward Drury and Robert Leslie, and they had robbed other Coventry people before, including the vicar of Allesley, the Reverend Bree, whose pig they had stolen. Before long, they and Baker had confessed everything. Although they had been carrying loaded pistols, they had not fired them at farmer Edwards or his friends, but had hit them with their pistols and with sticks, before robbing them of thirty shillings. It sounded like a dreadfully violent attack, and the robbers had left the dying man where he was, before running away and splitting the money between them. It was a shocking case.

In early April the men were put on trial and sentenced to death. Daniel heard his parents talking about the judgment later that day.

"This one's going to be different," his father was saying. "No trip to Whitley Common this time, where they do the usual executions – they're going to make an example of them, to warn other highway robbers and suchlike that Coventry will not stand for this sort of behaviour."

"Why, what's going to happen, then?" Daniel's mother asked, puzzled.

"Well, farmer Edwards was a tenant of Lord Leigh at Stoneleigh, and his lordship wants the men hanged on his land, to make an example of them. He's going to pay the costs of the whole trial, and for a gibbet to be set up, along by Wainbody Wood – you know, up there on the high road out of the city. Any traveller from that direction will see how Coventry punishes such men!" He smiled grimly. "And the talk is that Lord Leigh made the decision even before the trial happened – he at least judged the men to be guilty even before they could be proved innocent!"

"Well, it was quite clear that they were guilty, wasn't it?" said his wife, uncertainly.

"I suppose so," Daniel's father sighed. "But there's more: once the men are dead, they're going to hang their bodies in chains. These ones are not going to be cut up by the doctors for research, but left to rot where they hang!"

Daniel's eyes widened. Everyone was used to hangings, it was true, but this was something else. He ran off to find William: this time it was his turn to give some grim news.

***

Late April. Could it have been a wetter day? As the crowds made their way south out of Coventry, the long straight road stretched before them in a haze of rainfall. They could barely see ahead, as the trees dripped with the constant weight of water on their new leaves. The day was only just beginning to dawn, and the crows were already

67

swooping low across the sky, making a sound which seemed prophetic of the day's business. It was as if the very air was crying, thought Daniel, and well it might …

As his father had said, there had been other executions in the city, usually on Whitley Common, and Daniel guessed that there would be many more in the years to come. This, somehow, felt different. The place his father had described was known as the Three Mile Stone, being that distance from the city, on Stoneleigh Common. It was an unusual site to have chosen, and one normally to be avoided as it was a lonely and dangerous place. The spot where Lord Leigh had chosen for the hangings stood on a hillside at the highest point of the long road, before it swept down towards Kenilworth.

It was a long walk for the vast throng of spectators, who were as excited as ever at the prospect of a day's "sport". The city of Coventry had been buzzing for days. Three men were to be punished for a terrible murder, and two them were soldiers. Military men generally punished their own by firing squad, and it was rumoured that certain regiments billeted in Coventry thought hanging was a disgrace to the uniform – they might therefore try at the last minute to stop the executions. As a result, a regiment of the Scots Greys staying in Coventry had been sent elsewhere, so that they could not interfere.

Daniel and William shared the excitement. They were soaked through to the skin, but at least it felt like a holiday, even though it was just a Wednesday. Everywhere they looked they saw people they knew: it seemed as if the whole city had come out to watch. The rain was pouring down when they reached the top of the hill, but they, like everyone else, hardly noticed. They were waiting for the prisoners to arrive, and shouts could be heard from those at the back of the crowd, as they saw the procession approaching – sheriffs, constables and soldiers, guarding the wooden cart on which the prisoners stood.

Suddenly there was a hush. The crowd parted and the convicted men were wheeled into place at the foot of the gibbet. There were three separate ladders, on which each man would climb up to certain death. Nothing would save them now, though Daniel's mother and her friends had been on the lookout for a hare in the undergrowth. "What *are* you talking about, mother?" Daniel asked. Had she lost her mind?

"If a hare runs out from beneath the gallows, it's a sign that the Justices will be merciful, and not hang the men," she replied. "There's a wise woman in Coventry who has predicted it."

Scornfully Daniel and William turned away. What rubbish! They listened to the men who had reached the platforms at the top of the gallows. Already each had a noose around his neck, and each was speaking his last words on this earth, or so Daniel supposed; there was so much cheering and jeering that he couldn't really hear.

All was ready. The men awkwardly shook hands with each other as they prepared for the end. It only needed the ladders to be pulled away and the crowd would see what they had come for. Bizarrely, and to everyone's amazement, a small animal rushed out from the undergrowth beneath the gallows! It was a hare! Unbelievable! Had the prediction come true? The cheering got louder, and the sheriff stopped everything. Horsemen were sent off to find out if there were indeed any messages of mercy.

There were none. Before Daniel knew what was happening, the ladders were pulled away and the men were quickly dead. It was going to be a long, slow walk home, he thought, as it felt as if almost the whole population of Coventry was there, shouting and laughing at what they had seen.

On the way home, William had more information for Daniel. "He really can be a pain," thought Daniel. "He likes to feel important, I guess …"

But what William said – his all-knowing Mam had told him before they set out – made Daniel's skin crawl. The men's bodies were going to be taken down when everyone had left, and they were then going to be coated in tar to preserve them. They would be wrapped in a kind of harness made of chains, and hung up again on the gibbet, until the bodies eventually fell to pieces. It might take years before they rotted away, and all that time, anyone who approached the city from that direction would see them, and know that you didn't mess with the justice system in Coventry.

***

And it was so. Daniel never wanted to attend another public execution, though there were many more in the city. Years later, when he and William were old men with children and grandchildren of their own, the tattered remains of the bodies were at last removed. Only a rusty chain was left on top of the timber frame, and in bad weather you could hear the groans of the chain and the creaks of the wood as you passed by ...

CHAPTER SEVEN

Ribbons and Riot

In the early part of the nineteenth century Coventry had been famous for at least two centuries for the quality of its ribbon weaving. By then, between a third and a half of the population of Coventry worked as weavers, and most worked on hand-looms at home. In 1831 a ribbon manufacturer called Josiah Beck had set up a steam-powered loom at his factory in New Buildings, near Holy Trinity Church, and the home-based weavers, who were already underpaid, feared that this modern machine would take away their jobs.

Tilly hated being poor. She knew she wasn't really meant to live like this: when she looked at the beautiful silk ribbons the family produced, she knew that she really should have been born into a different family, one where all the girls wore beautiful dresses and decorated their hair with fabulous ribbons and bows. She had seen ladies dressed like this in town – and even girls her age – and she longed to be like them.

"You spend too much time day-dreaming," her sister Phoebe told her. "Just remember, some are born rich and others aren't … and we're the ones who aren't."

But Tilly couldn't help it. Her full name was Matilda, and she liked to roll the word around her tongue sometimes, and pretend she was someone else, living among rich and fashionable society.

"My lord, may I present Miss Matilda Bradshaw? She is the youngest of the family, her sisters Phoebe and Harriet will be arriving at the Assembly soon."

"Welcome, Miss Matilda," the handsome young lord would reply. "Would you care to dance? I am sure you must be much prettier than your sisters."

And so the daydreams would continue. Tilly was indeed the youngest in her family, which had been larger still at one time: her only brother Edward had died when she was a baby, as had another sister, Eliza. Tilly didn't remember either of them. Edward had "come to a bad end", apparently, and the family didn't speak of him. And earlier this very year her sister Hannah had died, still in her twenties.

Tilly's parents, John and Elizabeth, were weavers, just as their own parents and grandparents had been. Coventry, like the towns and country villages surrounding it, had been at the centre of the industry for centuries; whole families knew nothing else. Tilly's father's parents came from Chilvers Coton, in the north of the county near Nuneaton, and her mother's parents from Bedworth; all the relatives Tilly knew, in fact – uncles, aunts and cousins – worked the hand-loom.

It had always been poorly paid, there was no doubt about that. Usually the man of the house earnt most, with his wife bringing in a bit less, and the children the least. They worked from eight in the morning until seven at night, if their eyes could stand it as the darker nights came in. Still, they managed, and father was incredibly proud of their hand loom, which he treated with more respect than his children, so Tilly had heard her mother say!

John Bradshaw had brought his young wife to Coventry in the early years of the century, believing, like so many, that their prospects would be better in a big town. He had been a dreamer too, in those days, but his dreams had not worked out as he imagined. There were now so many weavers in Coventry that prices were kept low, and after the wars with Napoleon ended in 1815, prices went even lower. For the last five years cheaper ribbons had been imported from abroad, and there was less demand for the more expensive, luxury Coventry ribbons. Now the family lived in one of the "courts" in Much Park Street, right in the heart of the city. These were tiny cramped dwellings, huddled together in streets which had been there since medieval times. Many of the houses were centuries old, and were in poor shape: often there was no glass in the windows, and rags were stuffed in the window-frames to keep the wind and weather out. The children had to sleep many to a bed to keep warm. Harriet told Tilly that this was why Eliza had died – she had a weak chest, and the cold and damp had done for her. It was probably true, as Tilly had recently watched her dear sister Hannah become weaker and weaker, coughing until the blood came from her lungs.

Tilly and her sisters were determined that their grown-up lives would be different. Phoebe was already "walking out" with a young man, George, who came from a village south of Coventry. "I know he's only a labourer on the land," she told their mother, "and he probably won't ever be a rich man, but if I marry him I will live in the country and breathe the fresh air, not like the grime and soot here." Harriet was setting her sights higher: her young man, Joe, was an apprentice watchmaker to his father in Spon End, and everyone said that this was a good trade which was likely to expand. "You wait," she would say.

"One day we'll live in a proper house with a garden, and I'll have a maid to help me with the children!"

Their mother would go quiet when she heard these ambitions. If only they might do better than her! They had hoped as much when they had sent Edward to Bablake School, but he was easily led, and had fallen in with a bad crowd in town. She still loved John, but there had never been any prospect of improving their lives. Now, in fact, things were getting worse. For the last two years they had seen no increase in the price they could get for their goods. Some of the silk masters had been paying by the day, not by the item, and others were paying less than the usually-accepted price. She had a horror of being brought so low that they would have to go into the workhouse at the old Whitefriars. A silk mill had been set up there for the paupers to work at, and conditions were appalling: the master only paid the workers a penny out of every shilling earned, and kept the rest! She had brought her girls up to be respectable, too, and there were stories of drunkenness and goodness knows what other goings-on in the workhouse. She shuddered to think what might become of them if they couldn't keep going where they were, hard as it was.

Now, in the winter of 1831, they seemed poorer than ever. Tilly was permanently hungry. "It's because you're eleven," Harriet said, with all the superior knowledge of being thirteen. "You're growing and you need fuel!"

All the women of the household knew that John felt bad about their hardships. He had started going to meetings with other weavers, and the men were all in agreement that something had to be done: surely if they were reasonable with the masters, and told them truly how hard it was to manage, the masters would help? Wasn't it in their best interests, after all, to keep a healthy, skilled workforce? Coventry alone had more than five thousand hand looms, and Tilly had heard that about half of all the people in the city were workers in the weaving trade. How could they carry on like this and not starve?

Father had begun to come home and thump his fist on the table after some of these meetings. Two of his brothers and several cousins had been involved in trouble two years before, in Nuneaton, when one of the overseers had been pelted with filth; in the same year there were thousands of workers who went on strike – mother's brothers, who lived in Bulkington, had joined in. It seemed that matters were about to become a whole lot worse.

One Sunday evening in November, as they lay in bed, Tilly and her sisters heard their parents quarrelling.

"It won't do any good, you'll lose a day's pay if you're not at the loom, and some of the young lads could get violent," they heard their mother say. "It's all very well thinking you can be reasonable, but there are some hot-headed youngsters who will take matters into their own hands if you're not careful."

"It's a risk we've got to take, Elizabeth," their father replied. "We can't go on like this, as you well know. Tomorrow we'll meet the masters, and hear what they've got to say. All we want is to go back to the prices we had two years ago, that's not too much to ask. We've chosen a handful of sensible men to present our demands, so it will be all right, I promise."

"Sensible men! Demands! You need your heads looking at if you think the masters will listen to demands from the likes of us. We're ten a penny, and now that Mr Beck has that steam-powered engine loom set up, who needs as many workers anyway? The machine is going to take work away from human hands, don't you see?"

"Nonsense, woman," their father retorted. "We are skilled. A machine can't replace our delicate work."

And so the argument continued. Tilly had heard about this big machine, set up at Josiah Beck's ribbon mill. It could do the work of many hands. Tilly's job at home was winding the silk onto the bobbins while her mother was a warper, who loaded the long threads of silk onto the loom; her father then did the weaving itself. Her father said that machines could do all this work by itself, so what would happen to them, if all the masters decided to install machines and stop employing families like hers?

The next morning, John Bradshaw announced that the family would be stopping work at noon, and he would be going to a meeting in Cross Cheaping. He would hear no argument, he said, he wouldn't stand any longer for the masters to take the bread from his daughters' mouths. Shortly after noon he stopped the loom and with a quick peck on the cheek for Elizabeth, strode out. Elizabeth and the girls did not know what to do. Should they work the loom themselves? Should they go after him? Elizabeth was adamant that they should stay in the house; she expected trouble, there was no doubt about that.

Tilly was restless for the next hour. She could hear men's voices in the distance, she was sure. It was no good, she had to go and see what was happening. As she slipped away, she heard her mother calling, but she was determined. This was important.

The crowd in Cross Cheaping was much bigger than she expected. They were nearly all men, of course, and most of them young and, as her mother had feared, looking quite aggressive. They were waiting for the masters to come and answer their demands, but as yet, nobody had arrived. They sensed that nobody would.

"It's time we saw for ourselves what this machine is like at Beck's!" one of them shouted. "If it's true that it can do the work of many men, we're doomed, along with our wives and children!"

"Yes, and if it's as they say, there's only one thing for it – let's break it up!" shouted another, and before Tilly knew it, the whole crowd seemed to be surging forwards, pushing their way up towards New Buildings where the factory stood. She was looking for her father – where was he? She reckoned there must be hundreds of men there, and she couldn't see him. Was he going to be one of the loom-breakers? She shivered at the thought. She would have to tag along and hope that nobody noticed her. She needn't have worried; by this time the crowd was beginning to resemble an angry mob, with one thought on their minds – to smash the engine-loom.

Arriving at Beck's, Tilly could just about see the man himself come out of his house to speak to the mob at the factory door. Then all hell broke loose. Some men rushed the door, and though Beck shouted to his men to close it, the men had got inside. Shouts grew louder, and to her horror, Tilly watched as Mr Beck suddenly disappeared under a mass of yelling men, who were beating him with sticks! It was too horrible.

Suddenly Tilly was aware of her sister Phoebe beside her. "What on earth are you doing here, Tilly? This will not end well – we'll all end up in jail for sure. Come along home, Ma sent me to look for you."

"I can't leave now! Where's father? What if he's one of the men beating Mr Beck? Oh, I can't bear it!" Tilly replied, and broke away from Phoebe. She wriggled between some men, only to witness Mr Beck being knocked out, and his body thrown into the mud. They had gone mad! Some of them would hang for this!

Thankfully Beck appeared to revive, and Tilly saw one of the men pick him up and push him into his house. The crowd seemed to hold back at this point, when one of them, a young man Tilly recognised from one of the courts near her home, shouted, "Let us in to see the loom!" and the cry was taken up by the mob. Mr Beck was obviously afraid of so many of them at his door. Were his family inside? Tilly wasn't sure if he even had a family, but if so, they would be frightened too. The door was opened, however, and a great wave of men surged forward again, many of them disappearing into the factory itself.

All Tilly could hear for the next ten minutes was the sound of smashing glass and splintering wood. Stones were being thrown into the factory by the men still standing outside, and the men inside were throwing bits of machinery out of the windows, so that the air seemed full of flying debris. All at once, Tilly's heart nearly stopped: smoke was seeping out of the windows – they had set the mill on fire.

The crowd began to draw back now, as bits of the roof, ceilings and floors of the mill began to explode into the surrounding area. The fire had taken hold very quickly; half an hour later and the mill was no more.

Tilly decided to run. She could hear shouts from the direction of the market. Soldiers at the barracks had been called to quell the riot. What if they fired on the crowd? She ran as fast as she could, and only a few minutes after arriving, her father burst through the door too.

"Thank the Lord you're back!" Elizabeth cried. "I told you it would end like this! Get into a clean shirt, for goodness' sake, and let's get the loom working in case the law arrives. We need to look as if we've all been here all the time."

Quickly John did what she said. He looked shaken, white-faced, and more frightened than Tilly had ever seen him.

"I didn't expect this, Lizzie," he said. "It all happened so quickly. It makes no sense, no sense at all."

All was quiet outside that night. The theatres and pubs had been closed for fear of more violence, and there were guards standing watch over other ribbon factories in town. In the coming months seven weavers from Coventry were put on trial for "riotous and tumultuous destruction of machinery". Four of them were discharged, but three were sentenced to hang. One of them, in what seemed like a bizarre miscarriage of justice, was the young man who had helped Mr Beck get up after he had been knocked out. Eventually, and after many protests at the sentences, they were transported for life, one to Australia and the other two to Van Dieman's Land (present-day Tasmania.)

It was a terrible lesson for the weavers of Coventry – and for their masters, who did agree to start paying the price which had been in place two years before. No more steam-powered looms were installed in Coventry. In the meantime, however, other cities elsewhere continued to produce machine-made ribbons, and as the years went by nobody wanted hand-made Coventry ribbons any more. By the time Tilly was married, there was hardly any work for at least half the population, and soup kitchens were set up in St Mary's Guildhall for the starving and poor. Tilly and Harriet married watchmakers, men who were at the forefront of the new Coventry trade, and Phoebe married her country boy and settled in the green fields outside the city. But it was too late for their parents. Only ten years after the violent events of 1831, they died in poverty, and were buried, like so many of their weaving friends, in St Michael's Churchyard, with not a stone to mark their graves.

CHAPTER EIGHT

Moonlight Sonata

During the Second World War Coventry was already a centre of industry, and now turned its many factories into producing arms for the war effort. It was thus a target for German bombing. In 1940 and again in 1941 much of the city was destroyed by enemy action – the Coventry which existed before 1940 looked very different from the Coventry we know today. Most of it has been rebuilt, and the medieval St Michael's Cathedral has been left as a ruin, with a new cathedral now sitting alongside it. In November 1940 the Germans gave the codename Moonlight Sonata to their destructive raid, which lasted for over 11 hours on a bright moonlight night. Their target, Coventry, was clearly illuminated.

Sally thought how tired her mother was looking these days. Since rationing began, she had had to queue for several hours each day to exchange her food coupons for their meagre weekly supply – in January bacon, sugar and butter; in March, meat, and in July even tea had been rationed. The amounts available to each family seemed very small, and most people they knew had dug up the flowers in their gardens to plant vegetables instead. Some had an allotment to grow even more; many had started keeping pigs in the back garden! Sally's little brother, Peter, was always complaining about being hungry, probably because sweets were in short supply too. All of it was making Mum very weary, Sally thought.

It was over a year now since war had been declared, and Sally had seen so many changes in her short life already. Her older brother, Colin, was away with the Royal Warwickshires, and Mum and Dad were constantly anxious about where he was and what might be happening to him. School was going on much the same for Sally and Peter, but lots of their friends had gone away to the countryside, as evacuees. Coventry was full of factories, many of them turning out armaments for the war effort, and so it was thought to be a target for German bombers. Lots of Sally's parents' friends had sent their children away for their safety, but she was glad that her dad had put his foot down: "One of my children is away at the war," he said, "and I want the other two where I can see them. If anything happens here at home, at least we'll all be together."

It wasn't the most comforting of thoughts, but Sally supposed he was right. Her friend Alison was staying with a family on a farm in Gloucestershire, and wrote letters home saying that the lady there smacked her legs if she wouldn't eat the food, and she had to go to bed at seven every night. Sally reckoned she'd be home before long.

Not a lot had happened, anyway, at least so far, to suggest that Coventry was a dangerous place. There had been bombs dropped nearby, in a village near Rugby; that was in June, and at school they now had to practise wearing gas-masks. Mr Lee the headmaster had timed how long it would take for the whole school to get down to the cellars when an air-raid sounded.

At the same time Dad had prepared the family shelter. Some of the neighbours had built tin shelters in the garden, or even brick ones a bit like the pigsties, but one of the options was to kit out the space under the staircase at home. It was snug and warm, and meant they didn't have to go outside in their pyjamas. Mum, Peter and Sally could all sleep on a mattress down there, and Dad was often out on fire-watch, scanning the sky for bombers. The theory was that if the house was bombed, the staircase itself would provide shelter for those underneath it. Sally just hoped they wouldn't suffocate, but she didn't say anything to Mum, and certainly not to Peter, who was a bit of a cry-baby, in fact. Mum would read them a story by torchlight before they snuggled down, and it was quite an adventure, really.

In late summer Peter, who was a light sleeper, had been awake when bombs fell in the south of the city, and reckoned he had heard an enormous bang when one Sunday night the Rex Cinema in town had taken a direct hit. Fortunately nobody was hurt, and everyone had a good laugh when they realised that the film due to be shown the next day had been "Gone with the Wind"!

In August and September, though, Sally began to keep a little chart on the wall of the under-stairs cubby-hole, of all the nights when they heard air-raids going on. Mum cuddled her and Peter a bit more tightly than usual in their hidey-hole, as they heard planes buzzing overhead on their way to …. where?

In October, things got worse. One Saturday night, Dad was at home, as it happened, and it was only just dark. One huge explosion was what they heard first, and then several more. Then it went quiet. Mum prepared some supper of bread and cheese, and they heard the "all-clear" siren go at about 11 o'clock. Dad looked out of the back door, and said that he could see a terrific blaze somewhere in the north of the city.

"Come on, let's all go to bed," Dad said, and they all settled down - not in the shelter, but upstairs in their own beds. Sally was tired anyway, and soon fell asleep. Just an hour later, though, she felt the whole house shudder. A bomb had fallen in the next street, but hadn't exploded. The war was coming closer! It was only now that Sally began to feel that it was all too real.

Over the next few weeks quite a few bombs fell on the city without exploding, and one day Sally found Mum crying. It turned out that some brave men had been killed at Whitley while tackling the unexploded bombs, which had gone off.

That night Sally and Peter could hear Mum and Dad discussing whether it was time to send them away for their safety after all. Lots of buildings had been damaged in the city centre by now, including the home for old ladies called Ford's Hospital – a beautiful old timber building. Owen Owen, the main department store, had been hit, and the fire station had, too. Were they safe, living just half a mile from the city centre? How accurate were those German bombers – or did they even care about bombing just the factories – were they out to kill Coventry people too?

To Sally's relief, her parents decided they could stay. Finding accommodation outside the city was difficult now, as so many families had left. Colin had written too, sounding confident and saying we were winning. Sally wasn't sure if he was just trying to make her parents feel good, but perhaps things would be all right.

But it wasn't long before the chart on the wall grew fuller: air-raids were happening every night. In October some of the biggest factories were hit, and incendiary bombs started fires in large areas of the city.

Then came November 14th.

Peter wasn't feeling very well, that night; he had already gone to bed in the afternoon with tummy-ache. But at about seven o'clock Sally heard a loud cracking sound, and while her dad was checking the black-out they all saw a terrific flickering light, like lightning, coming through the black-out curtains. Her dad went outside to see what was going on.

"I think we'd all better go down under the stairs tonight," he said when he came back in. So Peter was hauled out of his nice warm bed and they all squeezed together under the stairs. Sally had the feeling that something worse than usual was about to happen. Her parents kept exchanging funny looks, and there were no stories tonight, just, "Try to get to sleep, both of you". Before they had gone into their den, Sally had seen the full moon lighting up the sky, and had realised that the bombers would have a clear view of the city when they came over. It was so bright it could have been day.

Sure enough, it wasn't long before it happened. A loud crash came, after a horrible whistling sound; some windows at the back of the house were smashed, and Peter shouted, "I can hear the big gun in the field – it's giving those planes a dose of their own medicine!" The din was deafening, then BANG! – it sounded as if every single window in the house shattered, and they heard the clattering of tiles falling from the roof.

"Don't move, Alan!" Mum cried, as Dad started to open the stairs door, but it was too late – he had disappeared into a cloud of thick plaster dust. Quick as a flash, Sally sprang out too, and followed him into the hall before her mum could stop her. "Sally! Come back here! It's not safe!" her mum shouted, but it was too late.

What Sally saw was unbelievable. The electricity had gone, but that brilliant moon shining into the house revealed doors hanging off their frames, and every window in the house was without glass. Her dad reached out his hand to her, and they picked their way across the dining room. He didn't speak, seeming calm, and Sally felt, in the silence once the brick and plaster settled, that she was sharing a special moment with him which they would remember forever.

Through the holes where the doors had been, Sally saw that the dining room was open to the air – the French windows had been blown in and were lying crazily across the table. They trod carefully across the glass-strewn floor into the kitchen. What a sight met their eyes! The plates, cups and saucers which had been on the dresser were all in tiny pieces over the floor. The most amazing thing was that Mum had left a box of soap flakes on top of the washing machine, and the explosion had split the box open, raining down white flakes all over everywhere – it looked like snow in the moonlight.

Gingerly they retraced their footsteps to the front door, and tiptoed outside. It was then that they saw that their house had no roof!

"Sally, I think we'd better get back inside," her dad said. "It's not safe out here." More planes were still coming over. Sally could see waves of them in the distance, making their way towards their target, Coventry, her home.

They scrambled back, over the debris in the house, and crouched again under the stairs with Mum and Peter. The night was very cold. It was about three in the morning when things began to quieten down, and it wasn't until six in the morning that the all-clear was sounded.

Daylight revealed just how badly their street had been damaged. Every single house had lost its roof, and two houses had been completely destroyed. There was rubble everywhere, and Dad's bicycle was under a heap of broken bricks and tiles.

It took a day or two just to clear up. Fortunately the electric and water supplies were all right, so Mum was able to see what she was doing in the short, dark November days, as she swept and tidied. The cooker was broken, but they had a camping stove. Peter soon stopped moaning when Dad cooked up a great dinner of fried bacon and eggs. They used up the whole bacon ration in one meal, but it was worth it.

Two days later, Dad returned from town and said, "Right you two, you're coming with me. I want you to see something you'll never forget." How right he was. Peter and Sally struggled down the road after him, not really wanting to see the horrible destruction as they approached the city centre. What met their eyes was amazing. There were burnt-out cars and trams everywhere, houses like their own with no roofs, and a heavy covering of dust and smoke choked their throats. A train had been blown off its rails and lay half-way across the nearby road, which, like many roads, was completely blocked to traffic. Their journey was hard as they clambered over the remains of fallen trees and chunks of broken tarmac.

Arriving in the city centre – or what was left of it – Sally felt suddenly confused. Familiar buildings had either disappeared altogether or had bits of them hanging off at mad angles over the road. There were soldiers clearing the roads, and people were walking about in a daze. Broadgate wasn't there! What? Broadgate wasn't there? It was true – the very heart of the city had been blown to pieces. Owen Owen was a shell, and only the tower of the Market Hall still stood, with its big clock now stopped. Everywhere else, as far as Sally could see, was a mass of half-standing walls and blown-out windows among the drizzle and smoke.

"Hurry up, kids," said Dad, "We need to get closer."

"Where are we going?" complained Peter. "I've seen enough. I want to go back!"

"Oh no, my boy," Dad said firmly. "We are going to the cathedral."

Sally looked up at the great spire, one of the famous three in the city. They had walked past Christchurch, and Holy Trinity had its great west window boarded up with black material. There was still a familiar slogan painted in white all over it: "It all depends on me, and I depend on God."

Suddenly there were more people scurrying in the same direction – why? Sally soon found out, as policemen appeared and a large black car made its way past, and stopped close to the cathedral.

It was only now that she realised that the cathedral itself had been bombed. Only the spire and the outer walls still stood. She could just see that the inside was one great heap of bricks and rubble. None of the pews were there, and none of the beautiful stained-glass in the windows. She could see a sort of pathway which had been opened up from the base of the spire towards the east end … and now Sally and Peter saw a man get out of the car, to be greeted by the mayor. Good grief – it was the king! How wonderful that he had come! Sally caught just a glimpse of him in the ruins, and saw that he was being led towards where the altar had once stood. Now in its place was a large wooden cross, made out of timbers, Dad said, which had fallen from the medieval roof. Later he explained that these timbers were found lying across one another, looking exactly like a Christian cross. The church mason, Jock Forbes, had seen it as a symbol of Jesus' sacrifice, and later the words "Father, Forgive" had been written at the bottom, to make an altar. He meant to show the world that although Coventry had been destroyed, it was willing to show forgiveness towards its destroyers – and one day it would rise again.

Peter was whining now. "I don't like it, Dad," he wailed. "It's too sad. Please can we go home?"

"You're right," said Dad. "It's wonderful that the king has come to comfort us, but I feel sad too. We'll build our city up again, though, don't you worry, and we'll be friends with cities all over the world again, especially the ones that have suffered like us."

It took a long time to reach home and they were all exhausted and shocked by what they had seen. Their city had suffered so terribly that in years to come the word "Coventrated" was invented to mean "completely destroyed". Dad had been right, as always – they would never forget what they saw in Coventry that day.

CHAPTER NINE

The Beautiful Game

Coventry City Football Club has only won the FA Cup once – in 1987. Thousands of fans travelled to Wembley for the Final that day, and thousands more watched it all on television. After the match, the city centre came to a standstill as huge crowds celebrated, even more cramming into town when the team returned triumphantly with the famous Cup, now decorated with sky-blue ribbons. That weekend, everyone in Coventry was a Sky Blues fan.

Amit couldn't remember a time when he hadn't been mad about football. His earliest memory was of hearing the thud-thud of a kicked ball, as he lay in his pushchair in the garden. His two older brothers, Pavan and Dev, made goalposts out of piles of crates from their grandmother's shop, with some old tarpaulin stretched over them. His mother would be screaming at them to be quiet and not to launch the ball into the next-door neighbour's garden. Dev, like their dad, was fanatical about Man United, and just to annoy them, Pavan had decided he was going to follow Liverpool. Amit had grown up listening to their arguments about who was the best centre forward, the best goalie, or the best defender. They had all the stats at their fingertips, and Amit, hanging on their every word like all kid brothers, became a walking encyclopaedia about league tables, top scores, and player transfers. It had become his party piece: "Go on then Amit, who was Chelsea's Player of the Year in 1976? Who came third from bottom in the League in 1984?" he would never disappoint: he knew all the answers and had got a reputation in the street for being "Little Mr Memory Man".

But it was all going to be different this year. Amit had decided he was going to be a Sky Blues fan. His brothers and his dad had cracked up when he had declared that Coventry City FC was going to win a trophy one day – "What for, kid, for wearing the shortest shorts? Brian Kilcline for having the curliest curls?"

Amit didn't care. While his brothers (Pavan was twelve years older than him, Dev ten) spent their weekend evenings at Tiffany's or Mr George's, meeting girls without their parents' knowledge and dancing to The Specials and The Selecter, – "Coventry's greatest!" Pavan said – Amit was reading up on football facts and storing them up in his head. He knew that this season, 1987, the Sky Blues were going to do something wonderful. Never mind 2-Tone, what Coventry did in 1987 would always be remembered.

The road to Wembley had started well: joining the Cup games in the Third Round, Coventry had beaten Bolton Wanderers 3-0 – a decisive win. But better was to come: in the Fourth Round they had been drawn against the mighty Manchester United – and they were away from home, playing at the hallowed ground of Old Trafford. Amit, a long-term follower of United, knew that Alex Ferguson's team was going to be hard to beat, especially at home. It would be like jumping an enormous hurdle in the Grand National. Could it be done? Dev and his dad were in their element on the day of the game

"Think the weedy Sky Blues can take on the likes of Peter Davenport? It'll be a massacre, son!" they had chorused. But they had gone very quiet when City had only gone and done it – they beat Man United 1-0, the first defeat in an FA cup tie for manager Fergie. The next three rounds had Amit heart-in-mouth as he listened to the scores at tea-time on his bedroom radio; he needn't have worried, City won them all, even if it was by a squeak in the semi-final.

And so the day had come. The day, if he was really honest with himself, Amit had hardly believed would really happen: Coventry City FC, his beloved Sky Blues, were going to Wembley! He didn't care about the fact that, as his dad said, their opponents were unbeatable – Tottenham Hotspur, of all teams to play, were going for a record eighth victory in the FA Cup. Spurs had never lost a Final. The Sky Blues had it all to do.

All week everyone at school had gone Sky Blue mad. Even the girls were excited. His teacher, Mr Jones, was an Art specialist and had made decorations for all the classroom windows, with posters of all the players holding cut-out trophies. I hope he's not pushing our luck, Amit thought. Paper chains in sky-blue tissue-paper had been strung across the classroom ceiling, with balloons in the corners in light blue and white. As Assembly began on Friday morning, the headmaster came into the hall to the tune of "Let's all sing together, play up Sky Blues"! It was amazing, old man Smith had never seemed much of a sport before, but there he was grinning from ear to ear as the whole school yelled out the song as he climbed onto the stage.

"I have a very special announcement today, children," he said, when everyone had quietened down. "You probably don't know this, but my brother is the manager of a television shop in town, and he has offered to set up a really big TV for us here in the school hall tomorrow, so that we can all watch the match tomorrow and not miss a thing. It will be like seeing the match at the pictures! What do you think – are you going to come?"

The noise was unbelievable. Even the teachers were cheering! Were they going to come? Obviously!! Amit had wondered if he would feel really part of the match if he watched it at home on their small set in the living-room. His grandmother had said she would close the shop and his auntie had wittily said "let's all watch together", but he didn't think he would be able to relax with the family round him. He knew he would want to shout and scream! His mum and grandma wouldn't be too keen on him doing that; he was always being told that his granddad, who spent most of his time in bed, would not be happy if there was a "damned racket downstairs", as he called it. And no doubt his mum would be interrupting all the time, asking if anyone wanted a snack, or walking in front of the screen to tidy something up. Pavan and Dev would be needling him on the sofa every time the play went against his team, and cheering Spurs on. So to watch it on a big screen in school would be brilliant! He would never have imagined his teachers would think of such a thing.

That night, Friday May 15th, Amit could hardly sleep. The local news on the telly had been entirely about the build-up to the match, showing the huge crowds of people who were travelling to Wembley the next day. Mercia Sound, the local radio station, had Sky Blue Fever all through the day and evening. At last, Amit drifted off to sleep...

The morning of May 16th began with bright sunshine. Amit woke to the familiar sounds from downstairs – his brothers still snoring after their night out on the town, his mum and grandma already up and cooking for the day ahead. He decided to slip out to the park and see if any of his friends were up for a quick game.

He had expected things to be quiet, still. But what met his eyes was amazing: all along the Foleshill Road there were sky-blue banners and balloons, and on the traffic island there was a huge "Play up Sky Blues" sign, surrounded by hundreds of blue paper flowers. The shops all had Good Luck banners pasted in the windows, or pages from last night's "Coventry Telegraph" showing the faces of all the players. When he got to the park he saw that the bandstand was covered in blue and white streamers. It was all so unexpected, Amit thought; until a few weeks ago it seemed that he was the only Sky Blues fan around … now everyone was suddenly mad for their own city's football team. With mixed feelings, he went home for breakfast.

The rest of that incredible day seemed to go by in a flash. Although kick-off wasn't until 3 o'clock, the TV coverage began in the morning and Amit joined his friends at school to watch on Mr Smith's big screen. He was relieved to be there, as his brothers had not stopped teasing him over breakfast. "I reckon it'll be 5-0 to Spurs," Pavan had said. "Yeah, all in the first ten minutes!" Dev had added. "See you back home before half-time, kid – no point in watching a massacre!"

The school hall was packed. Everyone had brought lunch but Mr Smith had laid on iced buns – with sky-blue icing! – and all the teachers were wearing team colours. They seemed as excited as the kids! But the TV scenes were what absorbed Amit: Wembley Stadium looked magnificent, like a great white wedding cake, and the number of people there was unbelievable: 96,000!

As the teams were introduced by the commentators it did look as though Coventry City were far inferior to Spurs, who had several players who played for England. Had Amit's calculations gone wrong? He had felt really confident before now, looking at the goals scored this season and the tactics that John Sillett and George Curtis, the managers, had used; they had got the team playing "attractive football", said the commentators, but would this be enough to win the Cup?

The match began. The school hall was alive with cheering, so much so that the first few passes were almost missed, until everyone settled down. But disaster! Just two minutes into the game, Spurs scored! A fantastic header went straight past Ogrizovic, City's keeper, and Amit felt as though his stomach was falling through his legs. He felt sick. His brothers would be unbearable tonight! He took a great gulp from the huge bottle of orange juice his mum had supplied him with. Keep calm, keep calm, he thought.

Six minutes later his prayers were answered. City scored! All level after just eight minutes! How could Amit bear another 82 minutes of this? But five minutes before the break, Spurs made a breakthrough and their number 6, Mabbutt, scored. 2-1. A third goal for Spurs and the match would be dead.

During half-time Amit helped himself to a couple more iced buns and a long drink. He didn't want to talk to anyone; he was too knotted up with anxiety. He sat quite still where he was, though lots of the others nipped out for a run round the school field. The second half began.

It took twenty minutes before Amit dared to dream again. That day, he said later, he witnessed the most dramatic goal he had ever seen, and in fact it was later voted one of the top ten goals ever scored at Wembley. City's number 10, Keith Houchen, saw a cross come towards him, kept his eyes on it and threw himself at the ball. With a diving header just six yards out he banged the ball into the net. It was utterly spectacular! The noise was deafening! Wembley went mad, and Mr Smith looked likely to have a heart attack!

Amit felt like pouring the rest of his orange juice over his head to cool off. He had broken out in a sweat and could feel his heart pounding. This was unbearable! "I thought football was supposed to be enjoyable," he muttered to himself, "but this is torture." He took another long swig and helped himself to another iced bun from a great platter that was being passed round.

And so the 90 minutes were up, and scores were equal. Extra time! There was no time to get up and stretch his legs before play began again, and Amit was feeling almost paralysed as he sat, cross-legged, staring boggled-eyed at the big screen. He was feeling queasy.

Gary Mabbutt: a name to remember in years to come. A funny name, Amit thought, but it belonged to a great footballer who had played many times for England. One of Spurs' best, he had already scored today. Now history took over: six minutes into extra time, and City's McGrath centred the ball from the right. Mabbutt was in the way …

"… and, and, and …" Amit could barely repeat the words to his granddad later on, "the ball came off his knee, straight into his own goal! HIS OWN GOAL!"

Hysteria. That was the only word for it. The hall erupted, kids were jumping and cheering and the teachers were roaring their heads off. Was it possible that the great FA Cup had the name "Coventry City" written on it after all? 3-2 to us! Yesssss!

The last minutes of extra time were like slow torture. "Please don't let them score, please don't let them score," Amit repeated to himself over and over. But the stuffing seemed to have been knocked out of Spurs. When the end came, and the world had gone crazy, Amit could hardly take it in. "The Sky Blues have won the Cup, the Sky Blues have won the Cup," he kept saying to himself, ignoring the kids in the hall who were leaping about all around him. He felt dizzy, and before he knew it he had blacked out.

In the minutes after the match ended, Brian Kilcline, City's captain, had led the victorious team up to Wembley's royal box to hold high the great trophy, now decorated with sky-blue ribbons. Amit, however, had been sitting in the headmaster's office with his head between his knees, being heartily sick into a waste paper bin. The humiliation! He was furious with himself. Had it been the iced buns or the orange juice? Or just the tension and excitement? He might never know, but the fact was that he had missed the climax of the day, when thousands of City fans in the stadium and all around the country had cheered till they lost their voices.

Later on he was told that his mum had collected him from school after Mr Smith had phoned. Had it been a lovely day? She had asked, and insisted he have a lie down in bed. Mothers, honestly! Despite being sick, it had been the greatest day of his life.

***

"How you doing, kid?" a head came round his bedroom door. Pavan was grinning from ear to ear. Dev and his dad came in too.

"Come on, get out of bed," his dad said. "We've got a treat for you. We're all going up town – can you hear the noise?"

Sure enough, Amit could hear a racket outside. Hundreds of car horns, and raucous singing. Looking out of the window he could see traffic jams! What was going on?

"We'll need to walk," Pavan said. "Everyone in town is heading for the city centre; we'll never get to the party if we take the car."

And what a party it was. The city was festooned with sky blue, the sun shone brightly, and thousands of people crowding into town cheered and shouted till they were hoarse. "Let's all sing together," thought Amit, grinning to himself. Coventry! Brilliant!

End Notes

There are so many stories about Coventry's history. It is a place once favoured by kings and queens; it is well-known for the way its industries have changed over time, from weaving and dyeing to watch-making, bicycles, cars, and aircraft. Above all, perhaps, it is famous as a place of peace and reconciliation: after the devastation brought by war and the destruction of its beautiful cathedral, the city "rose again" to become a vibrant multicultural centre.

In this book I have picked out just a few moments in time as a way of illustrating some of Coventry's back-story. There are many more I could have chosen. All the stories here are a mixture of fact and fiction. The background to all of them is real, and in some cases the story retells an event which really did happen.

The Lunt Fort built by the Romans just outside Coventry, is real enough, but my story of Marcus and his horse (story 1) is an invention; we now believe that Lady Godiva (story 2) was a real person, but her "naked" ride through Coventry is probably a myth. The trial by combat on Gosford Green really did – or didn't – happen, (story 3) but Matthew's experiences come from my imagination. The "mystery plays", which told Bible stories in dramatic form, took place over many years in Coventry, but again the heroes of my story, Margaret and Nicholas, are made up, set against the background of the famous "Shearmen and Tailors" play, with its even more famous song, the Coventry Carol (story 4).

Mary Queen of Scots really was imprisoned in Coventry, but the innkeeper's twin children did not, so far as I know, exist (story 5).The horrible hangings on Gibbet Hill (story 6) are only too true, but the two boys in the story are fictional.

I have used a real family from among my own ancestors, the Bradshaws, to tell the story of the weavers' riot (story 7), but I have no idea whether they actually saw what happened that day. Many of the details of the 1940 November Blitz (story 8) are taken from a real-life account of one family's experiences, but their names have been changed; everything in the last story (story 9) is true, but the narrator and his family are invented.

I have tried in this way to bring to life some important events and places in the history of Coventry, by seeing them through the eyes of young people. At the beginning of each story I have given a short background description to explain that moment in history.

Places Mentioned in the Stories

Chapter One: Friend and Roman

The Lunt Fort at Baginton is open for visits, where you can see the gyrus. See www.luntromanfort.org for more information.

Chapter Two: The Countess's Bargain

From Broadgate, to the left of Holy Trinity Church, are Lychgate Cottages in Priory Row. Pass them, turn left and walk across the walkway towards the offices of BBC Coventry and Warwickshire. Here the remains of St Mary's Priory can be seen. The Priory Visitors' Centre was constructed to tell its story.

Chapter Three: The White Hart

Gosford Green is on the east side of the city. Follow the road along Far Gosford Street and at Sky Blue Way you can cross to the grassed area where there is a small plaque marking the combat.

The Charterhouse is on the left as you drive out of the city along the London Road. Visit www.historiccoventry.org.uk for information.

Chapter Four: Out-Heroding Herod

Travelling east to west along Gosford Street and Jordan Well in medieval Coventry you would have crossed Much Park Street before arriving at the High Street and Broadgate. You can still do this today. Arriving at Broadgate you would then have continued along Smithford Street to get to St John's Church at the entrance to Spon Street. Today Smithford Street does not exist, and so to follow the route of the plays you would have to walk from Broadgate down the Precinct. Notice as you cross from Upper to Lower Precinct that on your right is Smithford Way, recalling the old name. At the bottom of the precinct you come out at the junction of Queen Victoria Road and Corporation Street, to see St John's and Spon Street ahead of you.

Chapter Five: The Queen at the Inn

The Bull Inn was in Smithford Street, which no longer exists. St Mary's Guildhall is in Bayley Lane, right next to the old cathedral. Visit www.stmarysguildhall.co.uk

Chapter Six: A Grim Warning

Leave the city along the Kenilworth Road (A429), crossing over the A45. At the top is Gibbet Hill, which once formed part of Stoneleigh Common. Wainbody Wood is on the left. If you turn left along Stoneleigh Road you will come out at Stoneleigh Village.

Leaving the market, the farmer and his companions probably travelled west out of Coventry via Spon End; the fields mentioned may have been near present-day Hearsall Common. Coventry Market and the nearby car park now stand where the soldiers' barracks once were.

Chapter Seven: Ribbons and Riot

Much Park Street was a much longer street than it is today, crowded with houses. Cross the road opposite the Herbert Art Gallery and Museum in Jordan Well and you will see the remains of a medieval stone house there.

Josiah Beck's factory stood near present-day Hales Street, where it meets Millennium Place – more or less opposite Sainsbury's! It was located on the River Sherbourne, which is still there, but is now underground, though there are plans to regenerate this part of the city, and reveal the river once again.

Cross Cheaping was once a main market area in Coventry (Cheaping is an old word for "buying and selling" and the Coventry Cross once stood here). Today it is at the back of Primark, facing Holy Trinity Church.

Chapter Eight: Moonlight Sonata

St Michael's Cathedral is the building most famously destroyed in the Blitz. Visit www.coventrycathedral.org.uk for visitor information.

Another ancient building which was bombed, Ford's Hospital, is in Greyfriars Lane (the building was once called Greyfriars Hospital). Walk along Hertford Street from Broadgate and you will see a gateway on your left which leads into Greyfriars Lane. Ford's Hospital is opposite.

Owen Owen, in Broadgate, was once the city's main department store, which is now Primark.

Chapter Nine: The Beautiful Game

Tiffany's and Mr George's were popular nightclubs in the city centre. Tiffany's has become the Central Library.

Foleshill Road is the arterial road leading north out of the city, and during the twentieth century became the vibrant centre of Coventry's Asian community.

Lightning Source UK Ltd.
Milton Keynes UK
UKHW020806291020
372446UK00007B/623